Travis I. Sivart

Tangled Skein

The Traveller's Inn, Book 1

Travis I. Sivart

Travis I. Sivart

Tangled Skein

The Traveller's Inn, Book 1

Copyright © 2024 Travis I. Sivart

All rights reserved.

ISBN: 9798879628708

Talk of the Tavern Publishing Group

DEDICATION

To the gamers and dreamers.

Table of Contents

1. Taproom Dancing

Cogsley flinched—as much as an automaton could—when the glass mug shattered on the beam of wood an arm's length away. Tiny shards of glass scattered and tinkled on the bar, and the light of the LED lanterns cascaded rainbows across the bartender's bow tie and spotless tuxedo.

The three-piece band—a fiddle, a flute, and a banjo—picked up the tempo of the tune and raised the pitch of the music to match the pitch of the brawl.

Golem FloorSweeper, the second automaton, shuffled towards the shards of drink ware—grumbling—the broom and dustpan scraping along the wooden planks of the floor.

"Cogsley," the golem's voice was slow and melancholy, "why do they do things to make extra work for us?"

"Because," Cogsley's voice was nasal and echoed through the glass dome that formed his head, "they are living beings, who have no sense of decorum. The same reason they track mud across my clean floor, spit everywhere, and use the privy. They think living means making messes."

Cogsley's glow-dome lit up, and he crouched to avoid another shattering glass. The bartender was mixing an absolutely toxic and horrid drink: The Hangman's Blood— a drink of stout or porter, blended with rum, gin, whiskey, brandy, with a splash of champagne to give it a bit of fizz. It was like a Long Island Iced Tea, but if you added a dash of a horror flick to it. It was attributed to a writer named Richard Hughes, who probably died from alcohol poisoning on the Earth realm sometime in the 1930s.

Darome the Gnome apparated on the bar, his hands waving while he chanted. The misty blue glow of an ethereal dragon—as long as Darome was tall—appeared in front of him, and darted forth. The magical wyrm opened its maw to engulf the fur-clad barbarian shouting a battle cry of 'Adrian' while swinging a barstool at the gnome's half-ogre companion.

The ancient predator's jaws went wide and snapped closed around the barbarian's outstretched fingers…well, two of his fingers…its meter-long body coiling around the warrior's thick forearm. The mighty, but tiny, beast squirmed and struggled, squeaking and growling, trying to take down the foe a dozen times larger than itself.

Durg raised his arm, and the furnishing broke into splinters as it met an immovable object. The half-ogre smiled, showing fourteen thick, wide-spaced teeth gleaming yellow in the amber light. The crooked grin hinted at untold tales of meat and brews.

The blue glowing reptilian illusion gnawed viciously on the northern warrior, as the man took a meaty ham-fist to the face from Darome's oversized companion. The barbarian flew backwards, crashing into a table.

Elementius, the scholar and Professor of Tidal Towers University of Magics, lifted his glass as his table crashed to the floor under the barbarian's weight.

"You see, Tilbert," the elder continued his diatribe, stroking his short, grey beard with his free hand, "the tribal tactics of domination of the Frost-Bitten Barbarians are well known. Direct confrontation and joy of battle. That's the essence of how they find meaning in life. They also dote on their lineage and ancestors, and will go on for hours about how their father did this, and their grandfather did that…"

The thin youth beside the older man kept clacking away on the fifteen keys of the brass contraption hovering in front of him. Tilbert, who probably had some aeifain blood in the mix, sniffled and pushed his glasses up from the tip of his pinched nose to the bridge. A notebook bobbed in the air to his left, and a puffy feathered quill skittered across the page. The pen kept scribbling notes about everything happening around Tilbert, while the acolyte attempted to capture every drop of wisdom his mentor pontificated. After all, that was why the old man paid him.

Cogsley sighed and slid the Hangman's Blood down the bar. The glass moved at an even pace, whirling and spinning to avoid bowls of nuts and pretzels. The vessel jigged to one side, swerving to dodge around glasses of various shapes and sizes, some of which popped and crackled, whiles others hissed and bubbled.

A gnarled hand stopped it, then grasped the mug's handle. Spinning on the barstool to face the room, Croaker Norge, in his stained duster and fedora, raised the glass in toast to the ruckus. He took a long pull from the mug, cringing and shuddering at the taste.

"Ya gotta be kidding me!" The dusky-skinned woman beside the codger muttered and glared around the room. "I should put a needler into each and every one of these people, so I can have a few moments of peaceable drinking. How's a lady supposed ta get soused with all dese animals howling and beating their chests?"

"Oh, Kitten," Croaker's voice was like gravel being spread on plywood, "boys will be boys."

"Ta hell with that crap," the woman growled, "dere's no excuse for dis behavior. Why'd dis fight even start?"

"The Kitten has teeth and claws," Croaker chuckled.

"Dat's right, and don't you forget it," Kitten raised her wrist, and quick puffs of compressed air were followed by two of the bar brawl participants falling to the floor with shrill screams.

It was a busy night in the Traveller's Inn, and it was fight night because Jack Tucker was nowhere to be seen, and that always made the regulars feel a bit frisky. The risk of repercussion was low when the proprietor was away.

Two observers lingered in a back corner of the establishment, whispering between themselves and pointing at combatants.

Wanderly stood on a table, his hand on Nomed's shoulder, and shouted encouragement at various fighters. The halfling flicked coins into the fray, the golden currency propelled by his snapping fingers as the money rested on his thumb, his elbow jutting forward, to help with his aim.

"Just the tip!" Wanderly yelled when a patron turned to glare at him after being hit in the head with a coin.

Nomed—a demon half-breed—watched the chaos with a bemused grin, leaning on his hand-and-a-half broad sword. People avoided involving the swordsman and mage in any fight in the Inn, but often sought him out for tasks or information.

The two were an unlikely pair, and in the past had been competitors more often than allies. But in the Traveller's Inn, they were often seen together…which usually meant trouble. The truth of the matter was that the two had engineered the current bar brawl, all for a bet.

The Traveller's Inn was a place where people from all over came to gather. And by all over, it really was from all over. Different worlds, times, realities, and even dimensions. The pub and hotel was an interdimensional nexus that had a dozen doors in and out that could open to an unexplored number of places. Professor Elementius had tasked himself with cataloging and categorizing all the realms the doors had access to, but he rarely left his seat and tankard to do the task. Well, except to sojourn to the lavatory for his constitutionals.

Membership was required to enter, and it wasn't easy to get a membership. It wasn't because the Inn had particularly high standards—as shown by the current crowd and its choice of entertainment—but rather because the establishment was a bit hard to find.

The exterior of the building always blended to match the environment it appeared in. And by 'appeared in', it was meant the Inn was a travelling sort of building, and wandered from place to place.

It never looked odd whenever it appeared in a world. Whether on the side of a road, in the center of a city, or at an oasis in a desert, it always looked like it belonged there. People never wondered where it had come from. They always assumed it had always been there. It was part of the charm of the place. The building had figured out long ago that if you looked like you belonged where you were, very few people questioned why you were there.

Membership wasn't as much of an application process, but more of the Inn choosing you to be allowed to enter. Some folks came in once, and never saw it again when they left. Others became regulars, and traveled with the Inn as it moved around the multiverse and various incarnations of creation.

The interior of the building followed a common version of physics, which included magic. The Inn could visit places with other natural laws, but it catered to a specific type of crowd. And that sort of crowd expected gravity to make things fall, light to shine, and drinks to be watered down when cheap and smooth when expensive. Since the customers expected such things, The Traveller's Inn accommodated its guests.

The current setup of the common room was, well, common. It had an extensive bar along one side, complete with a mirror behind it and bottles on shelves in front of the mirror. Taps were set in the polished wooden surface of the bar, and various mugs, steins, tankards, and stemware hung from racks above. Smaller cups and glasses were stored on shelves beside the collection of bottles behind the bar, or underneath the bar itself.

Cogsley was the de facto bartender, bouncer, and cleaning crew, assisted by the large, lumbering clay golem, Golem FloorSweeper. Various imps, drones, and barmaids delivered food, drinks, and other requested items to the two dozen or so tables and booths throughout the main room.

There was a back room with a couple of pool tables, a half dozen dartboards, and a single foosball table. Pushed to one corner was a lone air hockey table that glitched, so the pucks picked up speed and ignored gravity.

Another open doorway led to the kitchen, pantry, and back office; a stairway between it and a hallway leading to the privy led up to rooms for rent. The band was on a small, raised stage in front of the stairs.

The establishment, as a whole, had homey, dark-wood floors, beams, rafters, tables, chairs, and benches. Eight doors stood at cardinal points and their sub-points in each corner. Windows on the walls on each side of the doors showed various places that didn't match the other scenes outside the other windows.

A snowy landscape, a worked-stone cavern, a mountain sunset, a stormy ocean dancing with lightning, a star-strewn backdrop dominated by a swirling purple planet, and a medieval city were just some of the things that could be seen outside of the inn.

The interesting oddity of the doors was not everyone would see all the different doors, windows, or things beyond them. The staff, and most of the regulars, could but quite often people who were visiting for a one-off could only see the door that applied to them. It was a quirk of reality dictating someone's perception, or maybe the person's perception created their reality. Professor Elementius had talked about that at length and was often heard questioning if there were even more doors—or portals, as he preferred to label them—that he couldn't see.

The front door burst open; a figure silhouetted in a deep, electric blue light stood within the frame. The band stopped playing, except for the flute player, who was in mid trill. The note wavered for a few more seconds before dying out. The brawl slowed and ground to a halt, combatants hesitating with bottles or other various weapons poised over their chosen rival.

"Good evening, sir." Cogsley drew out the words.

"Hey, Cogsley," Jack Tucker stepped into the room, the door closing by itself behind him. The proprietor looked around the room. "What's going on here?"

"Bar fight, sir," Cogsley stated the obvious.

"Well, stop it. We need to clean up; we're about to have guests." Jack bent and picked up a chair, setting it upright.

Standing, Jack looked at the patrons of his establishment. The gathering was all staring at the man.

Jack was not much to look at. He didn't stand out in a crowd, or even in most people's minds. He was utterly unremarkable. He had eyes the color of eyes, and hair-colored hair. He was neither tall nor short, but somewhere in between, and appeared to be somewhere between his late twenties and his mid-fifties, depending on the lighting. He tended to wear non-descript beige trousers, a mildly wrinkled white button-up shirt, and an earth-tone, wide-brimmed hat that had seen plenty of weather.

Jack sighed.

"Come on, people," he clapped his hands, "let's get to it. Set this place to rights and watch the message board. I expect to hear the chime any time now, and you all know what that means."

"Dinner time, sir?" Cogsley asked.

"Time to make the doughnuts?" Golem chimed in.

"Time to get down and get funky!" Wanderly giggled.

"Actually," Elementius stood up, holding his tankard, "the chime means that a new job has posted, and a reward will be associated with it. It also is usually accompanied by someone new entering the Traveller's Inn for the first time, and that you cretins and ruffians should be on your best behavior."

"It means I need another drink," Croaker muttered and raised his mug towards Cogsley. "Barkeep, bourbon, and make it snappy."

"Okay," Jack rolled his eyes and sighed, "this place is set to rights in the next ten minutes or else everyone needs to pay their back bar tabs in eleven minutes."

Pulling a pocket watch on a chain from his pants, the proprietor checked the time.

A stampede of sound rose while Jack looked down at the timepiece and a dozen people began setting tables and chairs upright, picking up fallen crockery and drinking vessels, and cleaning up in general.

Golem began a slow circuit of the room, weaving between people and furniture, pushing their wide broom and gathering broken crockery and dropped food.

Imps launched themselves from their high perches, burlap bags of sawdust on their backs, performing dusting runs as they flew low to the floorboards. As Golem cleared the mess—guiding it to the wall with the hinged floorboard, where they'd push it all into the floor chute that led to the basement and the monster below who fed on such things—the imps layered the floor with the soft, absorbent, and slightly sweet-smelling sawdust.

Porters and bar maids cleared dirty tables onto trays and into wooden crates. Afterwards, another would come behind and set fresh silverware, napkins, and sugar and salt bowls in the center of each.

"Who broke the table?" Jack bemoaned, holding his hands towards the shattered remnants around Professor Elementius's and Tilbert's feet.

"That was I, sirrah," the blonde-haired barbarian stepped forward, a glowing blue dragon still wrapped around his forearm and gnawing on the silver ring on his finger with enthusiasm.

"And you are?" Jack sighed.

The man rose to his full height in front of the Inn's proprietor, jutted his chin into the air, balled up his fist and thumped it to his chest. The small, magical reptile curled around his arm squeaked, squirming to get out from between it and the man's bare chest.

Jack had to look up to see the man's face, doing so out of politeness, and so he didn't just stare awkwardly at the turgid nipples on the man's sun bronzed chest.

"I am Goonthur," the barbarian intoned, his voice taking on a reverent quality, "son of Watt the Strong, son of Gurgie the Beleaguered, son of Pock the Cruncher, son of Koshie the Bold. My father, Watt the Strong, fought in the Battle of Stones, overcame hordes of trolls in the Rock War, braved the perilous volcano Truktruk the Fiery, faced down the rampage of the Kobold Uprising of Wet Hill a score of years ago—"

"Okay, Goonthur, got it, great." Jack interrupted, holding up his hands to stop the flow of history from knocking him over.

The Professor cleared his throat, and all eyes turned to him. He raised his newly refilled tankard of ale and took a deep draught. Lowering the drinking vessel, he smacked his lips and blew the foam from his moustache with a puff of breath.

"The Kobold Uprising of Wet Hill," he began orating, "was actually just the poor, clever beasts trying to get away from their enslavement by the wizard, Blandish, not some great triumph. I expect your father didn't win a great battle, but instead was pursuing creatures who merely wanted to get away to freedom. Truktruk the Fiery sunk into the ocean, so I suspect your father was probably on a fishing skiff watching it do so. As for the 'hordes' of trolls in the Rock War—"

"What!?" Goonthur bellowed. "Who is this man who thinks he can know so much about my heritage, clan, and father?"

"That's Elementius, my dear Watt's son," Tilbert said,

pulling his shoulders back with the pride apparent in the language of his body and tongue.

A tinkling noise that sounded like a tuning fork trailing along thin glass tubes interrupted the conversation. The sound continued for three breaths, then ended with a dull, tinny bong that sounded like a cheap brass gong being hit with a soggy chicken leg.

The scenes outside the windows began moving, like the gods were rolling the backdrop off the celestial stage beyond. The scenery moved quicker, changing to forest, then desert, then a blizzard. It continued changing, faster and faster, a dizzying array of endless places and landscapes that zipped past the windows faster than the mind could follow.

The scenery stopped. One moment it was spinning like a child's top, the next it was still.

A small bell sounded from the east door, indicating it had opened, and all heads turned to see who would step through.

2. Mind Over Manners

Luna Rose stepped into the roadside tavern and inn. Lightning flashed, the muddy street behind her shown in a single snapshot of white. Everyone stared at the woman, shaking off the cold and wet.

She ignored them. It was always like this when she went into a new place. People never expected a powerful woman in leather and plate armor to step through their door.

"Why's it always like this every time we go into a new place?" Moist Manx moaned, stepping around the woman blocking the door. "Why do you always stop right in the middle of the doorway so the rest of us can't even get past you? I mean, come on, it's raining outside, and we're cold and hungry. Have some consideration for others."

"She just enjoys showing off for the locals," Mogits Hauser chimed in, stepping out from behind her on the other side and hanging his cloak on a hook beside the door. "You see, lad, she's got an ego the size of her..."

"Luna!" A booming voice cut off Mogits's commentary. "And Moist! And...yeah, Hauser, you too, I guess."

Goonthur stepped up and enfolded his arms around the priestess, lifting her off the ground and pressing her to his chest that gleamed with a sheen of sweat. A turgid nipple awkwardly pressed into her rosy cheekbone, threatening to slip upward and put out an eye. The small, transparent dragon peeked at the woman through the barbarian's golden locks, hissing.

"Stop that, you imbecile!" Luna growled, wedging an arm between her and the barbarian's chest. She pried herself free and dropped to the floor. "I am a warrior-priestess of Aretha, Goddess of the Hunt, so you should respect me. It's one of our main tenets!"

Goonthur had already turned away, reaching for the thin, pimply youth who was dressed in all black.

"No," Manx held up one finger, while looking down at a palm-sized gramophone in his hand, "the rules are no touching. We follow the rules, right, big guy?"

The barbarian nodded, grinning widely, as the greasy youth glared up at him through damp strands of jet-black hair, cranking the handle of the gramophone with two fingers, then holding it up to his ear. Thin, tinny music whined from the brass horn-like projection on top of the device.

"I'll take a hug, big guy," Mogits Hauser stood in front of the giant northerner, arms held out to receive the mass of affection.

"I'm sure you would...mage," Goonthur spat the final word and turned away.

The room burst into activity. Drinks clinked, conversation erupted, and all heads turned away from the newcomers as if they had never come into the room.

"Barkeep!" Goonthur bellowed, causing the small creature on his shoulder to duck back into his hair. "Drinks for my friends, and some warm grubs! We'll take a table near the fire, and keep the ale flowing!"

"I think you mean grub, sir," Cogsley drawled from

behind the bar, "but I will see if we can dig something up that will satisfy your indubitably questionable tastes."

The group settled around a table in front of the roaring fireplace. Goonthur dropped into a chair at the head of the table. He put both palms down on the surface in front of him, smiling at his adventuring companions. The magical creature on his shoulder preened its tail.

Manx slid into the chair furthest from the fire, hunching his shoulders and pressing the musical box to his ear, while glaring around the room from under his stringy bangs.

Luna huffed and sat on a bench, crossing her legs. She folded her arms across her steel breastplate. Reaching down and shifting the massive iron morning star so it settled on the floor beside her, rather than the handle sticking up, she looked around the room to see who was watching and judging her.

Mogits turned a chair around, dropped onto it, and folded his arms across the top of the back. He smiled at the barmaid sidling up to the group.

The woman held a tray almost as large as the tabletop above her head with one hand. Reaching up, she grabbed the four mugs and set them on the table, followed by a pitcher of ale, a straw basket of bread, a bowl of butter, a trencher of cheese, a bowl of fruit, and a stack of wooden plates.

She deftly avoided Mogits's hand, wound her way back through the crowd, and disappeared into the kitchen.

The mage rolled a large coin across the back of his knuckles, a sly smile on his lips, watching the room like someone sizing up livestock.

Goonthur poured and distributed drinks, and Luna picked up a pile of cloth napkins and silverware from the center of the table and passed them out.

The four settled back, piled bread, cheese, and fruit on their plates, and sampled the ale.

"Hauser," Goonthur said the name like he'd bit into a

bruised apple, "check the board. I've got it on good authority that the perfect job is due to be posted any moment now."

Smiling, Mogits stood and moved through the inn to a board—between the stage and the hallway to the privies—that was littered with messages and posts. The man stood to one side, scanning the board with practiced nonchalance, and looking around the room for potential marks.

It was a tough crowd in the Inn tonight, and an odd lot to boot. An old man sat at the bar chatting with a wiry woman with a steel arm; a bare-chested man with dark, wavy hair watched the newcomers at their table, a smaller man talking and waving his hands beside the first; a bespectacled scholar was explaining something to a younger man beside him at a table near the door; a gnome sat glaring at the magical blue dragon nuzzling Goonthur's ear, a huge man with a misshapen face grinning like an idiot beside him, eating some sort of pie with his hands; and various other patrons eating and nodding to the beat of the band.

Turning his attention to the message board, Mogits saw a small, clear crystal blinking a bright white light above a parchment. Leaning in for a closer look, the mage grinned and pulled the paper down.

"Romance?" Luna was saying as Mogits returned to the table. "That is ridiculous! I don't need no stinkin' romance. I am a woman of action, and don't have time for anything of that sort!"

"Spiders!" Mogits slapped the parchment in the middle of the table, amongst the steaming platter of roasted beast, bowl of boiled beets, and the trencher buttered potatoes.

The 'wizard' swirled his robes and took his seat again, smiling like the cat who ate the canary. He rubbed at his nose, which twitched with anticipation.

"What?" Goonthur jerked away from the table, raising his feet from the floor.

The magical lizard squawked in surprise, and scrambled for purchase on the warrior's bare shoulder.

Leaning forward, the barbarian daintily lifted the paper to look under it, the mini dragon leaning forward also and peering suspiciously.

"Where, Hauser?" he asked, holding the paper with two fingers.

"On the post," Mogits pointed at the sheet in the big man's hand.

The warrior dropped it and jerked his hand back, unconsciously wiping it on his fur skivvies.

"The job, and the best one up there I may add," Mogits smirked, "tells of a village plagued by giant spiders, who drag their people to an abandoned tower. It promises a rich reward, and all the booty we can loot from the tower, which once was home to a school of wizards."

Luna reached forward, rescuing the paper from the gravy bowl.

The band began a sad tune, discordant notes wafting through the air.

Manx tilted his head, nodded, and wound his miniature gramophone in the opposite direction. He clicked the button on the side, and the magical device began recording the song and adding it to the teen's repertoire of angsty music stored within.

The war priestess read over the posting and slapped it back down on the table.

"I think this is perfect!" Luna tucked an errant strand of strawberry blonde hair behind her ear. "People need help, and we can get a nice tithe for the church from the reward, not to mention the treasure we can scrape up from the tower. I vote we do it!"

"I'm in," Manx mumbled, fiddling with his music box. "Spiders are cool, and I'm bored."

"Well…" Goonthur forked a piece of meat and shoved it into his mouth, "Ivrf dumf frump weff shoulf beef toop haftsy."

"What was that?" Mogits looked up from filling his plate with beef and potatoes.

"I don't think we should be too hasty; we should look at what else is up there before we make a decision. And this isn't a voting thing; I'm the party leader and I get final say. And I say I should go over and pick something better from the board."

"Why?" Mogits smiled, cutting through a rare slice of meat. "We have financial reasons, and of course some altruistic reasons, too, to do this. And since when do we do what only one of us wants to do?"

The barbarian glared at the mage, the small head of the dragon looking back and forth between the two.

Manx snickered and popped a chunk of bread in his mouth when Goonthur turned his glare his way.

"Is it the spiders?" Mogits asked. "Because if you're afraid of spiders, then we should definitely go look for something else. We wouldn't want our fearless leader to be uncomfortable. After all, if we don't all have our heads in the game, then we wouldn't be at the top of our game."

Mogits smiled meaningfully at Goonthur and popped a potato into his mouth.

"No!" Goonthur blurted. "No. Spiders aren't scared of me. I mean, I don't have any issue with slaying spiders. They're vile creatures, that's all. And I've killed lots of them before, that's all. I just wanted something new to eradicate, not just some little annoying pests."

"Oh, they're giant spiders. Larger than dogs, maybe even the size of horses. That should be something worth adding to your list of conquests. Hairy legs, dribbling mandibles, poisonous fangs, and lots of beady eyes. It would be really super heroic if we did this. Your family's name would be glorified with this simple act of squishing some bugs."

The barbarian paled.

The blue-glowing reptile on his shoulder stroked the man's hair soothingly.

"They aren't bugs," Manx muttered, looking at Mogits. "They're arachnids. Like scorpions and ticks. I had a whole sheet of them pinned to my bedroom wall, and they were never on the roach, fly, and beetle sheet. Always on the other one, and much more dangerous than just bugs."

Goonthur swallowed hard, dropping his double tined fork to his plate, his appetite gone.

"Fine," the barbarian said, his voice cracking, "this sounds…great. Just great."

"Then we all agree," Mogits's smile widened, "this is the job for us. We should eat up, get a good night's sleep, and leave first thing in the morning."

"Great, just great," Goonthur repeated.

The dragon cooed, rubbing its head along the big man's jaw.

Dawn, after a good night's rest for most of the group, found the adventurers at the same table. A platter of fried eggs, slices of ham, and chili-fired potatoes sat almost empty in the center.

Golem FloorSweeper pushed a broom around the place, creating drifts of sawdust that the scatter imps flew down and redistributed.

Cogsley wiped down the bar, his dome head pivoting, searching for any spot he'd missed.

"Why not?" Mogits asked.

"Because it doesn't make any sense!" Goonthur slammed a fist on the table, causing the magical beast on his shoulder to flinch and hiss.

"It makes sense to me," Luna interjected, "we start by questioning the villagers, and gathering all the information we can before going to the tower. They may know something that would help."

"What could they know?" Goonthur ran a hand through his wavy locks.

The glowing blue dragon's gaze caught the movement, and it leaped playfully, bounding through the barbarian's hair.

"That their people are being taken by giant...spiders, and they can't do anything about it?"

The large man pulled the creature from his head, idly turning her onto her back in his arms and stroking her belly. The beast cooed and stared adoringly at the warrior.

"I agree with Goonthur," Manx muttered, "talking to people sounds boring."

"It secures our reward from the village," Mogits sighed. "We need them to know it's us going out there to save them. That way, when we show up dragging a bag full of dripping, poisonous, spider mandibles, they know we took care of their problem, not someone else. People have cheated me before, and I don't want it to happen again."

"Chelicerae," Professor Elementius yawned the word as he shuffled by, still in his bedclothes and holding a tankard of ale, "spiders don't have mandibles. Uneducated cretins."

"Besides," the mage continued before the barbarian could interrupt, "we need someone to tell of our bravery and honor in case we die. I mean, if we're killed horribly under hundreds of hairy legs of hungry spiders, someone needs to tell the tale."

"Hundreds?" Goonthur swallowed hard, swiped up his mug of ale, and emptied it in one draught.

"Good morning," Jack said, appearing beside the table, causing the barbarian to jump.

The group chorused greetings at the Inn's proprietor.

"I see you're setting out for the Tangled Web We Weave job," Jack said, "and I just wanted to let you know we have the proffered reward set aside in the back for when you return. We will also have other services available here at your disposal if you return."

"If..." Goonthur moaned, and his admirer snuggled into his chest.

"Sounds great," Mogits smiled up at the man, "and we're thrilled to hear it. But...is there any chance of us getting a small advance, you know, just some travelling money for supplies and whatnot?"

"Nope," Jack returned the man's smile, "no chance at all. But it will all be waiting for you upon return, including shares set aside for any funeral expenses of any who don't make it. Keep in mind, resurrection and regrowth of limbs costs extra."

"Great, just great." Goonthur offered a weak smile, the tiny dragon snoring in the makeshift cradle of his muscled arms.

Darome pouted, his diminutive frame slumped on the bar, arms crossed, and lip jutting out halfway to the end of his protuberant schnoz.

Durg patted the gnome gently, the half-ogre's huge hand covering his partner's entire back.

Cogsley wiped around the illusionist's feet, diligently removing each scuff mark to the countertop as Darome shifted.

"Excuse me," Jack appeared beside the two, "what have I told you about putting your feet on the furniture?"

"I mentioned that, sir." The bartender's tone was dry and condescending.

"Thank you, Cogsley. Darome, what's going on?"

The gnome looked up, his eyes large and glistening.

"That brute," the wee man pointed at the door, his voice cracking, "stole Blueberry!"

"Blueberry?" Jack looked at Durg for clarification.

"Bouncy blue lizzy," Durg grinned, happy to be part of the conversation.

"Wasn't that an illusion?" Jack cocked his head and wrinkled his forehead.

"Yes…" Darome sniffled.

"Aren't they supposed to disappear at the end of use, concentration, when the spell is done, or something?"

"Yes…" Darome nodded.

"Then how did Goonthur steal it?" Jack asked.

"I don't know!" Darome moaned. "That's what I want to know. And if anyone should be allowed to keep Blueberry, it should be me! I made her, and I should be allowed to have her as a pet. I work hard on my illusions and have never had one become real before!"

"Did you ever think maybe there was something in Goonthur that made Blueberry become real?" Jack put a hand on the smaller man's shoulder. "Maybe the guy really needed a friend. And you know the fairy folk specialize in enchantments. Couldn't maybe a wee fae have seen this and decided to take the form of Blueberry? Darome? Come on, now, you know illusions aren't real, so shouldn't there be another reason this happened?"

"Yeah," the gnome snuffled, "but it's still not fair. He's just a big, dumb barbarian with daddy issues. He isn't even nice; he doesn't deserve Blueberry."

"I know," Jack patted Darome, "but think of it this way…if he doesn't make it back, maybe Blueberry will come back to you."

"Oh, Jack!" The gnome's eyes lit up, and he leapt to his feet on the bar. "Do you really think so? Do you think the muscle moron will die horribly?"

"Um…" Jack verbally stumbled, "I didn't really say that."

"Whatever…somatics," Darome stepped forward, now eye-to-eye with the proprietor, and grabbed him by his shirt. "I just want my Blueberry back. Do you think there's a chance they could die? Please say yes, Jack. Don't tease me like this."

"Well, yes, it is a possibility, but—" Jack held up a finger to stop the gnome's celebratory explosion, "I hope they make it back. This mission is very important, and if they fail, it will cause a lot of problems for the Inn."

"Well, some things are worth the price," Darome smiled.

"And for all the regulars here," Jack stared at the small man pointedly, "like the Inn being decommissioned and grounded, or even possibly someone else gaining the lease."

"Oh," Darome deflated, "yeah, I guess that would be bad."

"Yes, it would be," Jack nodded. "Now, please get off the bar before Cogsley blows a rod."

"Please, sir," Cogsley drew out the words, "I appreciate your concern, but do not bring my personal life into this. I am just here to clean the mess left behind by unthinking, uncaring, unfeeling living creatures. My hobbies and pleasures outside of work need not be addressed."

"Cogsley," Jack chuckled, "you never leave. You're always here, even when I offer to give you time off."

"Yes sir," the automaton nodded, "indeed, you are correct, sir. I am a slave of my work ethic. Now, Durg, if you would kindly remove Master Darome from the bar top, I can get back to my drudgery which is my pride and joy during every moment I am here."

Travis I. Sivart

3. Not Going Back Home

The sun was shining, and birds were singing as the four approached the village, a dark forest looming behind the collection of huts and houses.

"Reminds me of home," Moist Manx said, hunching his shoulders and shoving his hands into his pockets.

"You must have had a horrible childhood, Moist." Goonthur checked the hand-and-a-half broadsword on his back again, then the long dagger on his hip.

"No, not really, it was okay," the kid shrugged, his pants bobbing with the motion, "and I prefer if you call me Manx. Moist is just a descriptor."

"Angry father? Abusive mother?" Goonthur asked.

"Nope, Mother always said I could be anything I wanted to, and Papa would tell me how proud he was of me when I did anything. They really wanted me to be a warlock, though, summon the Dark Lord and commune with the underworld and all that."

"That's sweet. I know parents can be judgy, always adding pressure and expectations. Did you hide your bug collections from them?" Luna asked.

"No, didn't need to," Manx sighed, "they'd buy me extra pins and canvas. Said it was worth it, because I might be able to help people with what I learned."

"Is that why you always dress in black?" Luna said sympathetically and put a comforting hand on his shoulder.

"No," he shrugged the hand away, "it's because it's slimming, and I was a chunky kid. Always had to wear husky-sized breeches and tunics."

"Ah, I see, Moist!" Goonthur crowed. "Then your parents locked you away, and refused to feed you because you were an embarrassment because you were a fatty! Gave you oatmeal without sugar until you slimmed down."

"No!" Manx shouted. "What is wrong with you people? Why do you want my parents to be monsters? I hit a growth spurt and got skinny. They fed me normal stuff and said they loved me no matter what I looked like! And it's Manx!"

They moved along the dusty road in silence for a while, then Goonthur tried again.

"So, they died horribly?" the barbarian asked.

"Oh, my gods! Really? No! They're still alive and running the family taxidermy business that's been handed down from my father's father and his father before them. All the local nobility purchases from them for their stuffed stags, filled pheasants, posed possums, and billowing bison!" Manx huffed and shoved his hands further into his pockets.

"Come on, guys," Mogits came to the defense of the lad, "he had a normal...hold on, posed...possums? People purchase posed possums?"

"Yeah, it's a favorite where I come from. Fighting possums, bathing possums, possums at tea, possums playing Parcheesi...you know, all the regular requests?" Manx shrugged.

"All the...regular requests?" Luna hesitated. "Are there not regular requests?"

"Yeah, you know how rich people are...they find a

trend, get one, then someone else gets one, and the next one tries to do one better. Soon the poor possums are an endangered species, and everyone is eyeing the armadillos, thinking they look like possums in armor."

The group fell silent again, small puffs of dust rising and falling with each step.

"My parents," Luna said, trying to fill the silence, "sold me to the church when I was a girl. Not because I was a girl, but because they got twelve silver for me, and they needed to eat."

"Really?" Goonthur looked at her. "You can get that much for a little girl? Were you pretty back then, or something?"

"What?" Luna spun to face the barbarian. "You know what? You really are a pig! Just because you don't find me attractive doesn't mean…just because they sold me doesn't mean…"

The woman fell silent, huffing and red-faced.

"He's intimidated by you," Mogits smiled.

"What?" Luna and Goonthur said at the same time.

"I am not!" The barbarian drew his shoulders back, thrusting out his bronzed chest.

"Sure you are." Mogits waved a hand at the man. "You ignore her, then you treat her like some doxie. You're clearly trying to dismiss her obvious worth and skills."

"I don't need you to defend me," Luna spat the words at the wizard.

"Of course, you don't." Mogits drew back, holding up his hands, then gestured at her. "Just look at you. It's obvious that you can defend yourself, and the rest of us, too, if it came to it. You're skilled with your weapon, trained by the priestesses of Aretha. You're well-armored and equipped, and have a great head on your shoulders!"

"Well, yeah," she said, "thank you, I guess."

"And it's a pretty head, too, no matter what Goonthur says." Mogits added.

"What?" Goonthur and Luna said together.

"Oh, look!" Mogits pointed ahead. "We're here, and the village sent out a welcoming party!"

A group of townsfolk approached. There were about a dozen of them, all wielding pitchforks or hoes, marching towards the small group with dour and distrustful looks.

"Whadda ya want?" The spokesperson was a gaunt man, tall enough that anyone would've looked up at him, if he wasn't hunched with years of hard labor in the fields.

Mogits stepped forward, gestured grandly, spreading his arms and smiling widely. "We're here to solve your spider problem!" The wizard said.

"Ahurm," Goonthur grunted, "I am the leader of this party, and I shall speak for the group.

The barbarian turned to the gathered committee of countryfolk.

"My dear peasants…" Goonthur began.

"Peasants?" A woman's shrill voice, tinged with age, cut through the greeting. "Why's he think we're peasants? Does he know us?"

"Naw, Meemaw," replied a thick man in a leather apron with arms like tree trunks, "he's just making assumptions, like they all do."

"I don't even know why we come out to greet them anymore." The elderly woman spat. "They're just going to die horribly. But at least it gets us a week or so respite from the spider raids."

"Indeed," a man gurgled, "it's like a sacrifice. Gives us a break. I still miss Jimmy, was sorry we had to stake him outside of town last month. He always told good jokes and was the best butcher we ever had."

"Marty was good," another man commented.

"Yeah, he was okay," gurgle-guy said, "but he always cut the mutton steaks crooked, and that made them cook unevenly."

"Excuse me…" Goonthur said, pausing for effect, to no effect.

The villagers continued to reminisce over lost

townsfolk and bad meals.

"People!" Luna bellowed.

Everyone fell silent and looked at the warrior priestess.

"That's better." She stood up taller, pulled her shoulders back, and put her fists on her hips.

"Now," the old woman said, "she's got presence. Really gets your attention. And look at that breastplate! Draws the eyes without thinking of what's underneath. The twins could be floppy, they could be full and pouting, or they could be twin pears staring at the heavens themselves, and we'd never know. Never even consider it."

The men of the village shifted uncomfortably, every single one of them thinking of exactly that. Except Burt, who eyed Goonthur appreciatively.

"We're gonna talk with her," the old lady said. "Go on, honey. Tell us what you want to say. It's okay, that side of beef you're traveling with will keep his beef flaps shut and let you take the lead. Won'tcha, meathead?"

"Uh," Goonthur mumbled.

"That's what I thought," the woman cackled.

Mogits giggled.

"Well then," Luna shifted uncomfortably, "let's see, um, where should I start?"

"Spiders?" Manx suggested.

"Yes," Luna nodded, "if we could accompany you fine folks to the town, perhaps we can settle with a nice tankard of ale and you can tell us what's going on here. The more we know, the better we'll be able to help you save your village."

"And maybe you can tell us a few stories?" The old lady grinned up at the priestess, showing all seven of her remaining teeth. "I bet you have a passel of adventures and deeds just waiting to be sung about by the skalds and bards!"

The elderly lady thrust her arm around Luna's, pulling the warrioress up against her bony frame, and tottered back towards the village.

"I'm Tiggie," the crone grinned. "Now, go on, tell me

more about what you want from us here in the delightful hamlet of Salami."

Hours later, in an inn that shared a common room with the stable, the adventurers sat on wobbly benches with clay mugs full of foaming brew. Flecks of black floated in the head of the ale, and may have been bits of dirt, dead bugs, or detritus from the long-used barrels in which the ale was aged for a minimum of seven days, and sometimes as long as a fortnight.

Tiggie, the village elder, settled sleeping arrangements for the party, ordered food, and stuck close to Luna every moment. Even for the frequent forays to the privy—which was more of a covered, outdoor trench with wooden beams set at two heights to help you squat to relieve yourself.

Bernie the blacksmith—who'd called Tiggie 'Mee-maw' earlier—was speaking.

"The spiders came from the sky," the man was saying, "floating down on clouds of webs. Now, I know we've all seen this before, every spring and fall. Normal spiders—and the ones here are far from normal—once they hatch, push out webs from their tiny little hineys, and the wind catches them like sheets on the line. They're carried away to land somewhere and do all the things spiders do, right?"

The crowd of villagers, about three dozen in total, cheered in agreement and raised their mugs. Every single person swallowed as much ale as they could, every time Bernie asked if he was correct in something he'd said.

The group had to follow suit, because of the age-old adage of 'when in roam mode, do as the roamers do, which is to follow local custom or risk being lynched.'

Goonthur swayed on his rickety bench, his massive form leaning far to one side, then backwards, threatening to tip the whole pew.

Mogits sat beside the barbarian, lending a helping hand

to keep the man upright. Also, unnoticed by the warrior or the crowd, switching mugs with the man so that the wizard never imbibed more than a few sips before needing a refill.

Moist Manx sat in the corner, leaning against the three slats of a fence that separated the livestock from the dining area. He pressed the miniature gramophone to his ear and glared at everyone with bleary eyes over the rim of a mug in his other hand.

Luna was still in the clutches of Tiggie, who refused to let the priestess out of her sight. Even when the old woman needed to visit the privies, she insisted that the younger woman join her. She claimed it was a custom for women to always go to the lavatory in groups. And that she needed help walking. And Luna's breastplate was a shining beacon helping her find the way to a better place.

"These beasts, though," Bernie continued, "they weren't like the other, normal little pokes of spiders that arrived in silky pockets of…silk. They were huge, and fell from the sky by the dozens. Which I guess is a good thing, because if it was hundreds like normal spiders, I don't think any of us would be here today, am I right?"

The crowd roared again, and everyone threw back their drinks.

"They scattered, some coming into our delightful little home of Salami, the others finding their way to the abandoned tower not too far from here." Bernie pointed in one direction, indicating where the tower stood.

Tilting his head and leaning precariously to one side, he spun and pointed in another direction. He smiled and nodded.

"They gathered there," he continued, "and we avoided the place. After all, there's plenty of woods in the other direction, and it wasn't near our crops. Live and let live, and all that."

"Or live, and don't die by poking the spider's nest. Am I right?" Mogits added.

The crowd cheered, and everyone quaffed their drinks

again.

Bernie frowned, unsure if that was proper protocol. With a shrug, he took a drink from his own vessel and went on.

"Soon, the spiders began hunting villagers. We lost Toodles, the seamstress. Ilky, the bobbin maker. And at first, we thought the things just targeted people associated with weaving. Maybe a professional rivalry type of thing, but then they took Winkey. Oh, poor ol Winkey. He was the Mayor and thought he could slay the monsters by setting fire to the tower.

"Well," Bernie struggled with the words for a moment, "he was wrong. He was caught in the blaze, but he didn't die. He made it back to town, and would have survived it, too. Except a half dozen of the things came and dragged him away."

"Magic!" A new voice cut through the man's story, and the crowd looked up with a gasp.

"Oh, fiddlesticks," Tiggie muttered, "not her again."

A middle-aged woman in fine clothes that had seen better days—about a decade ago—stood in the doorway of the public house. Her hair was pulled up in a matted bun of twisted dreadlocks wound around themselves.

"I am Wilhelmina," the woman chanted in a sing-song voice, "and oh, the things I've seena…the future and the past, dangers in spiders as they massed."

"Is this all going to be in rhyme?" Luna asked, leaning heavily on Tiggie.

"Yup," the old woman sighed and nodded, "and she won't stop until she's finished, so we just let her go on."

"Uff," Luna moaned.

"Women and men have died in pain," the newcomer said, "in light of day, or dark of rain. Let me 'splain, how the spiders reign…"

"Get to the point of the tale," Mogits sang, the crowd looking towards him, "we'll all agree you're right, and drink some ale!"

"As the wise wizard said," she continued, "I'll tell you how the people end up dead. The tower of magic has called to the beasts, and they gather souls to it as treats. For the real monster lies within, and is a prisoner in his own right, and that is where the tale did begin.

"But heroes did come, and they did fall. No one conquering the evil, until y'all! As we gather tonight, you shall free us, am I right?"

The woman fell silent.

After the briefest of pauses, the crowd went wild, cheering, stamping, clanking clay mugs, then all fell silent to empty said mugs.

"So," Mogits's voice rose in the quiet, "does anyone think we can get a few things to help make your prophetess' words come to pass?"

Hours later, Goonthur leaned against Mogits, fetid breath stinking of bitter, underaged ale, and his words slurred.

"I gotta bring...glory," the barbarian hiccupped, then continued, "to my family's name. I'tsh not eashy, either. Man, they expect a lot. I gotta kill thingsh, not die, and do other thingsh."

"Fascinating," Mogits said, leaning away to avoid the spittle flying from the party leader's mouth.

"You're a good friend, Mogshits." Goonthur grinned, leaning in and closing the distance between him and the wizard. "I called you Mogshits, which is like Mogshits, but I said Mogshits inshtead of Mogshits. Oh, and hey! You can be Mogshits-faced! But I digreshs, ash I was shaying...you're not a good man, you're a bashtard. But you're a good friend. I shee how you looked out for everyone, even if you're a fraud."

"Did your daddy love you, Goonthur?" Mogits asked.

"He only wanted the besht for me," the big man threw

31

an arm around the wizard, "but I could never live up to hish reputation. It wash hard, living in the shadow of shuch a great man. He was amazing, always beating people, and thingsh."

"That was all said in past tense, my muscle-bound companion. Has he gone on to a better place?" Mogits asked.

"Naw," Goonthur drew the word out, and warm, moist air washed over Mogits' face, which scrunched up under the effort. "Um, what wash I shaying? Oh yeah! He'sh dead. But he went on to that great feashthall in the shky. Like, you know, he'sh drinkin shtuff with the god'sh and banging versionsh, vurguns...ver-gins! Yeah, vergins. Because he'sh great."

"Yeah, I know what you meant." Mogits looked around for help, or a way out from this unexpected bonding session with a man who outweighed him by almost double.

Luna had left with Tiggie, the offer of a more confortable place to sleep tempting her away from a corner in a stable slash common room slash straw covered and ale-stained floor of a public house.

Moist Manx was curled into a crescent shape against a sheep, sandwiched on the other side by a watery-eyed mule. The beast of burden blinked at Mogits, and the wizard wondered if he could switch places with the creature without Goonthur noticing.

But it was interesting to have the barbarian pouring his heart out to a 'drinking buddy' who'd had less than two mugs in the past six hours.

Mogits had slipped the noose of spilling his own background and history. It was always astounding to him how easy that was to do. All you had to do was ask the right question, and suddenly, the person asking you was telling you all about their worries, past, concerns, hopes, or dreams. It was always about them, without fail.

The wizard didn't mind though, not really; it allowed him to gather information without revealing anything about himself. And that was always better.

Wasn't it?

The big guy droned on, talking about his childhood: how he trained with swords since his fifth birthday; killed his first beast at nine; slew his first marauder at fifteen (to the disappointment of his father, who thought fifteen was much too late); and struck out on his own by eighteen.

The barbarian had so much pressure on him to do something great, and soon, that it boggled Mogits.

Why didn't the big guy just raise the one-fingered salute to everyone, tell them to bugger themselves, and go live his own life instead of trying to fulfill everyone else's expectations of who he should be?

It took more than an hour before Mogits could escape the disturbing bonding ritual. Once he had though, he had enough information, dirt, and knowledge of the man who thought he led the group that the wizard could have ridden that pony until the cows came home.

But Mogits knew he wouldn't use all the infortmation he learned, at least, not much, and not often. It was better to be selective in such things.

To abuse it would be to lose it. And Mogits never lost it. Not more than once, and that had already happened once before, a long time ago.

Travis I. Sivart

4. Towering Consequences

The sun made Goonthur wince. The barbarian's head pounded, and his stomach twirled in a slow, stumbling dance of too much ale and a greasy breakfast. Sausage and wine were not the best way to start a day after drinking into the wee hours.

And Blueberry was back. The small, glowing dragon was flying around the top of the tower that loomed above the group. Goonthur wasn't sure if anyone else could even see the creature, but she was a sweetie, and she was sweet on him.

He'd woken with her snuggled up next to him, a vibrating cooing noise coming from her. It even looked like she was smiling in her sleep—not an easy thing for a reptile.

During breakfast, she was nowhere to be seen. Being that she wasn't longer than his arm—and only as thick as Moist's skinny biceps—the barbarian assumed she was out hunting rats, or whatever she ate. Or maybe she just didn't like being around people.

Blueberry was a visually interesting dragon, not like the ones that Goonthur knew about from myth and legend.

Instead of being built like the traditional version of dragons, she was long, slim, and sleek. She also sported an adorable set of thick whiskers, which twitched with emotion and intelligence.

"Reminds me of this one time I rescued a princess with really long hair," Mogits stood with his hands on his hips, staring up at the tower, "she had a really stupid name, but she was great in…a pinch."

"Mhmm," Luna sighed, "a pinch."

"I'm bored," Manx said.

"Weird music and lights, right?" Mogits asked.

"Hm? What?" Luna turned to look at the wizard.

"That's some of the weird stuff Tiggie mentioned, lights and really weird music, right?"

"Glowing lights bobbing in the trees and maniacal songs were her exact words, I believe," the priestess corrected.

"Weird, but cool," Manx muttered. "I hope we see some."

The kid hated being called Moist, Goonthur thought. *The kid said it was a descriptor, speaking of how he crept into things unnoticed, like moisture. Just a name they gave him, back when he was in a gang, in the port city of Miasma.*

And that's exactly why Goonthur called him Moist. Words had power, and if he could use the right words, then he'd have power over the person they applied to.

"You okay, buddy?" Mogits's voice cut through the big man's thoughts.

Goonthur twitched when he realized Mogits had directed the question at him.

What the hell did I say to him last night? the Barbarian wondered. *Geez, I can't remember all of it, but I remember telling him about Woofie, and Elsie. She was a big girl, but she taught me so much. I would have run away with her, too, even though she was five years older than me, and practically an old maid. The things she could do with…*

"You alright?" Mogits' hand on his arm jerked him

from his reverie.

"Gravy!" Goonthur shouted.

"Frontal assault…boss?" Mogits added the last word as an afterthought, and it didn't sound like the term held the respect it was meant to convey.

The tower was tall-ish. It felt squat and short, but that's because it was so wide. It's fifteen meters of height—a respectable height, not even counting the gazebo-looking thing at the top—was underplayed by the fact that it was almost as wide as it was tall. The illusion—ugh, that word bothered Goonthur, he hated magic and everything that came with it—made the structure seem shorter than it really was.

The trees around the building were stunted, twisted, and withered. Webs draped from them, dozens of white silk cocoons dangling from branches and swaying in the breeze.

Blueberry darted between them, diving and twisting through the air. She stopped to inspect one, poking at it with a claw, and tasting it with her tongue.

Some of the human oubliettes were thin and swung more freely, and the barbarian knew whatever was inside had been drained of all liquid. Bile rose in his gullet at the idea.

I am NOT afraid of spiders! He thought. *They're just icky, and no one likes them. Well, except Moist, but he's a freak. And maybe Hauser, but he'd say he likes them just to piss me off.*

"No," Goonthur said, pushing Hauser's hand away from his arm, "we don't assault. Moist, go check the door, see if it's trapped, and then see if it's locked. If it is, open it. If it isn't, open it. I'll be right behind you, ready to kill anything beyond it. Luna, get ready to apply healing spells, as needed. Hauser…ugh…just make yourself useful."

"You got it, boss!" Mogits said cheerfully, pulling various things from pouches and pockets.

"I am not a healing priestess!" Luna complained, causing Goonthur to wince at her whiney tone. "I am a warrior priestess, and I shall be prepared for battle."

"You don't know any healing spells?" Manx, stepping towards the door to check it, hesitated.

"Well, I know some. Healing is part of battle, and to go in without that ability would be asinine. But it's more like a combat medic, not a healer! Don't expect healing, even if I am well versed in it!"

"Yeah," Manx sighed and continued forward, "got it. If I get poisoned or crushed, you might help, or you might attack the trap. Perfect."

The rogue crept towards the door, and Goonthur thought the kid looked ridiculous sneaking in broad daylight.

Did thieves look that stupid when creeping through dark alleys, preparing to stab someone in the back? he wondered.

Manx knelt in front of the entry, swept hair from his eyes, and ran his hands across the flagstones, pressing and pulling on the flat parts and edges, respectfully.

Blueberry flitted over, zipping around the doorway. She inspected the area, then darted upward to check the windows of the tower.

Finding no trigger points, Manx stood and moved to the doorframe. His fingers danced along the stout beams framing the entrance. After checking all the outer parts, his hands moved to the seam between the door and frame.

"Wizard," Goonthur growled at Mogits, "use your magics to check for magical traps. After all, this was a school for your kind."

"Oh yeah," Mogits waved away the suggestion, "already did. It's fine. The kid is doing great."

"You sure?" Luna was on the balls of her feet, morning star in her hand, tense for any upcoming battle.

"Oh yeah, no problem. It's all good." The wizard smiled.

"Clear," Manx stood and shouted over his shoulder, "except for the spiders in the tree line, there's no threats here. No pressure plates anywhere, and no spring poison things in the lock."

"Did you unlock it?" Mogits asked.

"What?" The thief turned and looked at the wizard.

"Did you unlock the door with no traps, Moist, or do I need to kick the damned thing down?" Goonthur growled.

"There is no lock." Manx sighed, shrugging, "It's barred from the other side. If it had a lock, I would've popped it, and then opened the door. I'm not some dumb backwoods moron who drank all night and doesn't know how to do his job."

"I can do it!" Luna shouted, planting her feet to charge the door.

"No, woman," Goonthur said, "save your strength for calling upon your goddess for healing spells. I'll open the door."

The barbarian swept the priestess back with one arm, causing her to stumble.

"He knows I'm a warrior priestess, right?" Luna growled to Mogits, recovering her balance.

"Enh," Mogits shrugged, "I'm not sure if he knows what day it is, so I think I can honestly say…maybe?"

The barbarian slammed into the door a breath after the wizard's answer.

The barrier exploded inward, shards and splinters of wood scattering into the interior darkness, followed by the roaring form of the warrior.

Blueberry darted inside after the man, a squeak of concern rising into the morning air.

A descending scream came from inside. A sharp 'wah' followed by a 'hoo-hoo-hoo' echoed off the stone structure's interior and was trailed by the dull thudding sound of the barbarian hitting something that was probably in a downward direction.

The remaining companions traded looks, then all three turned to the shattered entryway.

"Shall we go check on his landing?" Mogits asked.

"I guess…" Manx mumbled, shuffling forward. "He should've just kicked it. You never know what's—or what isn't—behind a door."

"I would've never made that mistake," Luna scoffed, following the rogue. "I would've so bashed the door down with my morning star and been ready for whatever came at me."

"Bashed the door down?" Mogits asked, picking up his pace to stay abreast of the woman. The priestess nodded. "With a spiked ball on a stick?"

The woman nodded again.

The three crossed the threshold, Manx first, then Mogits and Luna together. Darkness enfolded them, but the dimly lit interior came into focus in moments.

The wizard and priestess bumped into Manx, his arms spread out to stop them, his hands touching their junk. Though, later, Mogits would question if the young man had given a quick squeeze to one or both of their packages.

The ground fell away in front of the trio, the broken boards rotted away. About two meters of planks around the perimeter of the room was all that remained of what had once been a sturdy wood floor.

High-pitched, panicky screams from below let the others know where the barbarian had gotten to. He didn't sound hurt, but he sounded like he had something urgent on his mind.

"Spiders," Mogits chuckled.

With his chin, he gestured at thick webs connected to the walls of the ground floor and descending into the basement below.

The thick webbing created a funnel-like structure that ended five meters below on the stone floor of the lowest level. Above them were rafters that showed the second floor was still intact.

To the trio's immediate left were stairs that hugged the wall, leading up.

Mogits waved his hand at the stairs. "Should we go up, or help our fearless leader, who has taken an unfortunate tumble to the lower levels, which appears to be inhabited by spiders of various sizes?"

"Kitchen," Manx pointed straight across the open area of missing planks, then gestured to the right, "and the main fireplace. The chimney probably goes all the way to the top. Anyone see if there was smoke coming out from above? It will let us know if anyone lives here with the spiders. I would. Spiders keep the riff-raff away."

All three leaned down to look at Goonthur.

The barbarian was struggling, his arms and legs tangled in the sticky webs quickly enclosing around him as he inadvertently burrowed his way deeper into them.

Blueberry hung in the air above Goonthur, coiled into a tight knot, hissing at the moving shadows.

Huge eight-legged creatures skittered along cones of web hallways fashioned using the viscous strings. The architecture was beyond anything any of them had ever seen a spider weave—including Manx who'd made an intensive study of trap-door spiders.

"So…" Luna drew out the word, "down and save the moron, or up and beat the crap out of anything up there?"

"Um…" Manx debated.

"He might be of use if we bother to save him." Mogits pointed out. "He might—might—even be grateful."

"Ha!" Luna looked at the smaller man. "You know he'll just make excuses, or blame you. But…you're right. Let's go save him."

"Whatever…" Manx muttered.

"Wizard," Luna took charge, "burn the flames. Manx, anchor a line so we can get back up. And I'll…"

The woman leapt into the darkness with a battle cry to her goddess.

"Aretha!" she shouted, disappearing over the edge.

Mogits looked around, then at what he held in his hands. Shrugging, he tucked the items back into various pouches and pockets and pulled out new things.

Glancing at Manx, who was hammering a piton between stones of the wall, the wizard took a swig of something from a metal flask and spit it in a spray on the webbing nearest him. Striking flint to steel, sparks leapt from the objects, the webs melting, flames rolling downward into the brightening darkness.

Manx tied a coil of rope onto the metal spike he'd lodged into the wall. The younger man threw the coil over the edge, watching it unwind and slap the floor below.

"You go down," Mogits shouted, "help them. I'll keep doing my magic stuff to burn the webbing so the spiders can't hide from us!"

Manx nodded, drew a dagger, gripped it in his teeth, wrapped the line around his wrists, and rappelled down.

Mogits held the flask of oil, waving it around, and walking the circumference of the first floor. Pulling a torch from his backpack, he doused it with the flammable liquid, and struck the flint and steel to light it.

Making another circuit of the room, the 'wizard' applied the open flame to the oil-soaked webbing. The thin threads flared, and wandered in a downward wave.

Looking over the edge, Mogits's breath caught.

Luna was a blur of motion. Her morning star crushed one spider as she spun to smash in the head of another.

Manx was in a crouch, slinging short throwing knives with amazing precision. Blade after blade skewered the heads of the arachnids, the beasts skittering backwards trying to escape the attacks. The creatures crumpled to the ground, dead, legs curling under them.

The priestess frothed at the mouth, a thick foam of rage spraying from her lips as she raised her weapon of choice over her head and ran from one monster to the next, bashing them to lifelessness.

Mogits pressed his lips together and nodded approvingly. "That woman can kill!" the mage mumbled.

Goonthur was standing now, singed, and smudged from the flames that had freed him from the web. He smacked at his body, doing an awkward dance that didn't seem to be as much from the burning, but the fact that the icky spiders were everywhere.

Small spots of black were moving across the barbarian's body, showing that the gigantic spiders weren't the only ones inhabiting the basement. The warrior slapped at his chest and arms, whimpering. His sword hung from his back, forgotten.

Within a few minutes, a dozen enormous spiders lay upside down, legs curled to their abdomens.

Luna stood, shoulders hunched, panting heavily, her eyes dark and haunted but glaring into shadowy corners, looking for something to attack.

"We good?" Mogits shouted down.

"Yeah," Manx appeared from the shadows, clutching a bulbous mass, "I got the cephalothorax, pedipalps, and chelicerae from a Agelenidae Giganticus! This will be great for my collection!"

Goonthur turned and vomited, all while still doing that special dance that told of things creeping and crawling across his body.

"Great?" the wizard called down. "Look around for anything shiny that might be of value and get back up here."

In the time it took the others to get back upstairs, Mogits looked around the remaining rim of flooring that had once been the ground level.

He pocketed a few pouches from skeletons of previous adventurers and was dazzled by the set of kitchen knives he found. Using one of the few spells he actually knew, he discovered the blades were magical and would never rust or dull.

"Gin-soo," he mumbled, reading the inscription on the flats of the implements, "maybe djinn construction?"

Grunts from behind alerted him the other three had joined him. Mogits turned to see them pulling themselves up the rope.

"Why didn't you just use the stairs?" Mogits gestured to the door beside the kitchen that had fallen away to reveal stone steps leading down. He tucked the knives into a sack as his companions looked where he'd pointed.

"Mogits…" Goonthur growled, stepping towards the man.

"No," Manx stepped between the two men.

Goonthur looked at the smaller man who blocked his way to the spell caster, his eyebrows shooting up. Blueberry darted behind the thief, looking him over like she was sizing him up to decide if she could take him.

"Listen, you stupid sack of muscle—" the thief spun a knife, the blade glinting in the dim light spilling through the door and the single torch that Mogits held, "—this guy did his thing. And he did it well. Don't go spilling your masculine machismo onto him because you're scared you didn't. Being a man isn't just about being tough, it's about doing what needs done when it needs to be done. So, back off and get your head straight, okay?"

"Hey," Luna touched the barbarian's arm, and the big man jerked to look at her, his eyes wide, "it's okay. I rage. I know what comes with that. The pressure of needing to prove your worth. I battle with that every damn time I talk to you. I get it. Calm down, it's what you have to do every time you have that beautiful, wonderful surge of power that comes with crushing your enemies, seeing them driven before you, and hearing the lamentations of their women. I get it. So, take a deep breath, and calm the hell down."

"Fine," Goonthur breathed out heavily, "I wasn't going to do anything. But if that damned mage hadn't been jerking off up here, and had done what he was here to do…"

"He did do that," Manx spat. "Sso suck it up, buttercup, and let's see what horrible things are waiting upstairs. We got some good loot from below, and it'll spend well. I think I'm gonna buy a nice coat with my share. What about you three?"

"I have some split leather straps on my armor that need repairing, and a new morning star wouldn't do me any harm," Luna added.

"Sure," Goonthur growled, "whatever. I'll rent a bard

to write a ballad about my battle, or something."

Blueberry landed on the barbarian's shoulder, gripped the man's ear with one clawed hand, and petted his hair with the other.

"I can lead the way upstairs," Mogits grinned. "Of course, if I am in the lead, whatever is up there may kill me before we even see the second floor. But I'm willing to do it."

"No, I've got this!" The barbarian puffed his chest out and stepped towards the stairway.

"Of course you do," Mogits said, gesturing towards the steps.

The party moved to the next level, the small dragon standing on Goonthur's head, pointing the way upward with a talon.

Mogits lit the torches set into sconces as they moved along the meter-wide stairs, and light flared every three paces. At the top of the steps, he jammed the torch into an empty sconce.

The next floor opened before them, daylight streaming through a dozen unshuttered arrow slits on the walls. Luxurious accommodations spread throughout the single, large room: a wide bed with silk sheets; dark wood wardrobes hanging open to reveal robes and clothing that spoke of wealth; and furnishings that told of wasted money.

Lines on the floor showed where the room had once been divided into many smaller rooms. Small beams of wood jutted up from the floor where beams supporting walls—long gone—dotted the area.

The thing that really caught their eye was the woman who stood almost three meters tall, with six hairy, spindly arms. She wore a long, diaphanous gown that shimmered in the torchlight. Her short-cropped, dark hair was interspersed with more than a half dozen shiny, black orbs that darted towards the group and followed their every movement.

The woman opened her mouth, her bottom jaw

spreading downward and apart, and began to sing. The sound was like nothing they'd ever heard.

5. Sights & Sounds

Visiting the Traveller's Inn for a brief check in, we find Cogsley leaning down with Jack, Wanderly, and Nomed staring into the crown of the bartender's dome. Colored fog swirling under the surface of the glass.

The automaton was a special thing, and no one really knew where Jack found him. Some think the proprietor rescued him and brought him home, others whisper that the Inn itself created him. All Jack knows is one day Cogsley was greeting people at the door, hanging up hats and coats, and doing some light cleaning. Before long, he was delivering meals and filling room requests. And shortly after that, he'd moved to bartending and pretty much running the Inn.

Allow a moment to describe Cogsley in detail—something which hasn't been done yet—as it may help clarify things. Standing on two pants-covered legs that ended with shoes, and having two sleeve-covered arms ending with gloved hands, most people think nothing of Cogsley at first glance. His tuxedo with tails, white gloves, red bow tie, and other finery was what most people noticed right away. But it's the automaton's head that really gathers attention once people get around to looking at his face. But Cogsley had noticed, oddly bemused, a surprising amount of people never look at other people's faces.

Cogsley's upper knob is a smooth, transparent globe that almost always has a top hat perched on it, a simple but elegant hat band made of deep blue silk circling the crown. See what happened there? There's a good chance you noticed the top hat, and slid right past the fact that you can look through Cogsley's head and see someone standing on the other side of him.

The bartender's dome was in the shape of a huge, incandescent lightbulb, with the socket threads disappearing into the collar of his starched shirt. Within the glass confines of the noggin stands an arch of coiled wire that lights up when something is going on. It was the automaton's equivalent to showing an emotional, facial response. But, fun fact, it also lights up when he gets an idea.

Right now, though, Jack was tapping on the glass which is Cogsley's head.

"Nothing's clear. I can't make anything out." Jack said.

"Is this thing on?" Wanderly giggled.

"Lights are on, but…" Nomed began.

"That shall be well enough of that, sirs," Cogsley interrupted. "I assure you that your humor is top-notch and clever, but there is a slight chance I have heard each of those jokes more than once."

"Can you project it on the big screen, Cogsley?" Jack inquired, pointing at the sheet hanging in front of the stage where the band had been last week, when the adventuring group had been there.

Oh, that's another thing worth mentioning—and Jack loves to debate the topic—time is not constant nor universal. It varies from place to place and, frankly, from time to time. It's often a matter of perspective, just check theoretical physics for more on that. The point is, though less than a day had passed for the group in the tower, a week had passed for the folks inside the Inn.

It didn't always work that way, though. Sometimes folks would return after a month, and only hours had passed in the Inn. Perhaps something to do with the phlogiston (sometimes called aether, or in more scientific, formal circles some equivalate it to dark matter or dark energy), that the building was constantly enveloped by, or just a quirk of magic. The second theory was usually used, because it's much easier to discount natural—but little understood—phenomenon to magic, than trying to explore it enough to understand it.

"Oh boy, movie time," Croaker muttered from a booth in a dark corner.

"When did he get here?" Nomed asked.

"Duh," Wanderly elbowed the demon-mix-breed, "you're not the only one who comes and goes without being seen."

"Yeah, but he's an old man with no magic. How the hell does he do it?" Nomed squinted towards the shadows the gravel voice had come from.

"Come on, Cogsley," Jack took the bartender's arm and guided him around the counter, "ignore these jokers, and let's get you set up."

"Of course, sir," the automaton drawled, "nothing more I would like to do at the moment than be a spectacle for all to gawk over. Thank you so much for allowing me to be a projector. This is like a dream come true."

The two moved to the center of the common room, the others bustling about to move tables out of the way and set out bowls of popcorn, pretzels, and peanuts.

"Why do the good snack foods always start with the letter 'p'?" Wanderly wondered aloud, pointing at the bowls.

"Pickles," Nomed suggested.

"Potato chips," Jack added.

"Pistachio ice cream," Croaker muttered from the back of the room.

"I'm not sure if that counts, old man," Nomed said

over his shoulder.

"Don't be a pistachio hater," Croaker mumbled, "and buy a shirt, man. No one wants to stare at your bare chest all night long."

"Some ladies—and gentlemen—might disagree with that," Jack said, adjusting Cogsley's position, then moving to straighten the sheet on the wall.

"I think it's a very nice chest," Golem droned. "I wish someone had sculpted my chest as beautifully as his."

Inn employees moved about, filling mugs and tankards, and Croaker's wine glass.

"Okay, I think we're ready. Everyone grab a seat and settle down." Jack made a downward motion with his hands.

"Yes sir," Cogsley moved to sit.

"Oh, that dry wit, Cogsley," Jack said, "not you, my friend. I'm afraid you'll need to remain standing."

"Of course, sir. What was I thinking? The job of a bartender, therapist, manager, genius, and projector is never done." Cogsley resumed his bent position.

The automation leaned towards the screen slightly, and they could hear the whir of gears in the anticipatory silence of the room. The light from the bartender's glass dome brightened, then projected onto the white cloth in the front of the room.

A scene of five people appeared, and cheers and applause filled the space.

Goonthur, Mogits, Luna, and Moist Manx stood in front of a willowy woman with thin arms (covered in short, thick hairs) who gestured like an opera diva.

"Is there sound on this thing?" Wanderly asked.

"Ah, no." Jack said. "But…Golem, would you do the honors? Read their lips and tell us what they're saying?"

"Yes, I would be delighted," the construct said with their usual melancholy enthusiasm.

Golem thumped across the floor and stood next to the screen. In a moment, the figures on the screen gained voices, thanks to the assistance of the construct.

Shrill trills cut through the air, the spider woman raising her six spindly limbs as the pitch rose. Gesticulating towards the ceiling, the woman's body writhed in jerky motions. Her gown clung to her form, showing a smooth torso, an extremely thin waist, and a bulbous bottom half. The woman's legs were short and thick, ending in stunted feet with three thick toes.

Blueberry raised her head, her high, reedy voice warbling counterpoint to the song. The woman's gaze followed the creature as it launched itself off Goonthur's shoulder and circled the room. No one else paid the dragon any attention.

"Not very good, is it?" Mogits winced.

"There's no vibrato, and she's a bit flat." Luna nodded. "I'm not a brilliant singer, but I could do better than this."

"Ugh, my inner ear!" Goonthur shoved a finger into his ear, wobbling it around. "It's kinda making me nauseous. Anyone else's head spinning?"

Mogits reached up to touch his ears, wiggling a finger in the canal.

"I kinda like it. It's…haunting." Manx mumbled, winding his music box backwards. "Don't be haters, people. Everyone expresses themselves differently, and at least she's doing it. I can't say that for any of you. Judgy much?"

The group stood there, staring, transfixed—except for Goonthur, who moaned and thumped the side of his head with the butt of his palm.

"Nope," the barbarian moaned, "I can't take it anymore."

Drawing the enormous sword from his back, the big man took two steps forward and fell onto his face, his weapon clattering across the floor.

Manx didn't notice, still cranking his miniature gramophone as he watched the woman with wide eyes.

Luna glanced towards the noise of the blade, her brows knitting in annoyance, then back to the woman, her mouth hanging open.

The spider woman continued to sing, moving her head so her six eyes took in her captive audience. Her lower jaw, now separated into two individual chelicerae, moved from side to side in anticipation of a meal. Thick palps peeled away from her jawline, like rogue sideburns that got bored and decided to explore their surroundings.

She moved forward, her lower set of arms dropping to the ground, so she moved on four legs rather than two. More than a half dozen joints showed on each limb as the gown drew back, dragging along the floor.

"Hrmph." Mogits, hands in his pockets, leaned forward and looked to one side and then the other, checking the expression on the faces of his two companions who were still standing. "Looks like they're out."

The wizard rocked back on his heels and considered the situation. He took one slow step to the side, watching to see if their unexpected hostess noticed. The woman focused on the other three, approaching them, still keening her mesmerizing tune.

"With them out of commission, they'll never see me loot the room, or argue with me over anything I find," he said to no one in particular. "On the other hand, if she decides to feed on one instead of just being a wrapper I could lose one. Might not be a bad thing, if she goes for ol' meathead, but it would suck—heh, literally—if she decided to start with the kid or Luna."

The woman stepped past Goonthur, two of her four hairy feet stepping on him, moving towards the other two immobile victims.

"Well," Mogits sighed, "I guess the choice is a no-brainer...I'll search the room unless she begins to slurp one down like a pudding!"

The mage grinned and sauntered across the room, stifling a whistle so he didn't pull any attention from the woman. He stepped into the center of the room, which was now behind the woman, and began chanting.

"Hernde durnde, urp…bork, bork, bork," he mumbled under his breath.

Pulling small components from a pouch, he dropped a pearl into a pewter chalice and poured wine over the top. Lifting the cup to his lips, he tossed back the drink, then spit the pearl back into his hand and dropped it back into the pouch he'd originally pulled it from.

"Always makes the wine taste richer when I do that," the mage muttered.

He took a long pull from the wineskin, then dropped it and the chalice into his backpack.

"That always gives me confidence. It's like magic!" Mogits snickered.

The wizard waved his hands, his fingers winding into arcane configurations, and words of a language that twisted the minds of lesser beings flowed from his lips. One of the few spells he knew fluttered into existence.

Looking around the room, two distinct glows came into view. A smoking jacket hung on a peg on the side of the second wardrobe, and something hidden in the shadows underneath the bed.

"That's it?" Mogits grumbled. "This damned tower was once a school of higher learning for the arcane. Then again, that may have been an exaggeration. Like most magic is…"

Looking up, his magical sight revealed that dozens of things within two meters of the floor above were of a magical nature.

"Hellz yeah, beeches!" he squeaked. "But until then, let's get the goods. Bet I can find all the hidden loot before she even kills one of them!"

Mogits moved across the room and removed the silken garment from the hook, admiring it.

"Hm, looks like this one will make me comfy in any weather, and I'll look pretty snazzy to boot," he nodded and smiled. "Bet they'll notice if I'm wearing it, though."

He tucked it into his backpack and moved towards the bed.

Glancing over at the singing spider siren, he saw she had completely wrapped Manx in a sticky silk from head to toe. The kid lay on the ground, twitching within his viscous sarcophagus.

"But how's she singing if she's encasing them in icky, sticky stuff…" he trailed off as he turned to Luna.

The matron of the house was holding the woman aloft with four arms, spinning her. A hairy protuberance jutted out from underneath the gown, spinnerets moving together and away like pinchers, and a fine white substance spraying from the woman's abdomen.

"Very cool," Mogits muttered, then cringed, "but pretty damn…ew!"

Squatting next to the bed, the mage tore his eyes from the scene and looked underneath the frame of the massive furniture.

A pair of purple footwear sat underneath, toes curling up and ending in tiny, golden tassels.

"Slippers!" Mogits slapped a hand over his mouth as the word slipped out. He continued, quieter. "Now I can slip in and out of places without making a sound!"

Sliding off his shoes, and slipping on the slippers, he looked over to check on the lady-of-the-house's progress. The priestess was nearly enveloped.

"Hrmph," he grunted. "She works fast. Only a minute or two before she's done with the dumb one, then she'll be coming for me. Guess I better make this quick."

The rest was easy for Mogits, and decades of practice allowed him to scour the room in less than three minutes. During that time, he acquired a small coffer of gems and various purses and sachets of coins.

Turning to see what was going on in the rest of the room, he saw Goonthur was almost completely encased.

"Okay, time to save everyone." Mogits heaved a sigh,

then shouted, "Hey! Six eyes!"

The humanoid spider turned at the sharp sound of his voice. Something blue and wispy darted across Mogits's vision, causing him to turn and look for whatever it was. That's when she tackled him to the floor.

Mogits's high-pitched scream of surprise rattled the sconces on the wall, and the mage pitched heels over head as the creature barreled into him. The woman clutched him in four hirsute appendages, dragging the man upward as she pressed him to the wall.

Pulling the grappled mage onto the ceiling six meters above the floor, the woman's jaw divided. Saliva, in ropey veins, strung from one side to the other as she thrust her face towards his neck.

Reaching across his body, Mogits twisted the ring on his finger, and uttered three distinctive and simple words that rang with arcane power, "Bippity, boppity, boo!"

A stream of flame issued from the palm of the hand with the magical band; the alien creature screamed in pain and it enshrouded her with a fiery burst. The hairs on the monster curled, her skin crusting, then rupturing under the onslaught.

Mogits pushed himself further against the wall, attempting to draw away from the intense magical heat he'd generated. He found himself falling towards his captor—and the floor—as the woman lost her grip on the ceiling. The world moved in slow motion. The wizard watched as the woman's eight limbs, each with seven joints, released him and shuddered inward towards her body.

He smiled in triumph…a moment before he crashed to the floor on top of the blazing husk.

The mage screamed, only to have the air knocked out of him as he slammed into the age-hardened planks of the flooring. He rolled to one side, his robes dancing with small fires, and struggled to draw air into his compressed lungs.

"Unnngh!" he groaned, his vision blurring as his oxygen supply ran out.

A small, iridescent, elongated dragon flew into his range of narrowing vision.

It's a female, he thought, even as his body struggled to breathe. *But how can I tell? Magic, probably. Like I was ever good at that, though.*

She looked at him, cocked her head, drew back her lips in a growl, and blew out a cone of blue sparkles across the mage. His breath came back in a rush, relief quickly following. He smiled up at his miniature savior. Then Blueberry spit on him, turned her tail towards him, and lifted it. He saw a small, scaley flap at the rear of the reptile's belly convulse, and then the dragon disappeared from his sight.

Mogits sat up, grimacing at the sudden taste of musty thickness in his mouth. Slapping at the spots of dancing flames along his sleeves and chest, he put out the sizzling remnants his enemy had bequeathed upon him.

Hurriedly turning to the side, he saw that the woman was curled into an oddly polyhedron-looking ball, twitching as the last of the spell died out.

Looking in the other direction, Mogits saw Luna's cocoon, Manx's cocoon, and Goonthur mostly wrapped in the spider's silk trap—large puncture holes in his throat where she'd injected the paralyzing venom—and one eye staring in his direction.

Jerking backwards, the mage tried to decide if the barbarian was conscious or not. The eye of the warrior didn't follow his movements, but it was staring directly at him.

It would probably be okay. He hoped.

Ten minutes later, the priestess, thief, and warrior were freed of their bonds, sitting up and leaning against the bedframe.

"…a combination of wine, a sharp blade, my own cleverness, and my indomitable magic rescued you," Mogits shouted, his voice louder than it should have been, "you're welcome!"

"Hmmw wherb whoo esshhea fhew shee?" Luna asked.

"What?" the wizard yelled, leaning forward and cupping an ear.

"Hmmw wherb whoo esshhea fhew shee?" Luna asked again.

"Oh, hold on…" Mogits held up a finger, then stuck it his ear, doing the same to the other ear with his other hand.

Pulling out thick plugs of wax, he smiled at the groggy priestess.

"Sorry about that," he said in a normal tone, "I pushed these in when Goonthur said her singing made him feel bad. What did you ask?"

"You didn't think to warn us?" the priestess growled.

"Wasn't time," Mogits shrugged, "and I bet you wouldn't have listened anyway—you were way too into that chick's diva gig to bother to listen to some pissant mage you barely trust, and definitely don't place any value onto his skill set. Any other questions?"

Travis I. Sivart

6. Healer Who?

Blueberry sat on the shoulder of her beloved. The powerful man's muscles rippled underneath her imaginary claws. She drew herself out, stretching around his neck, so her head poked out one side and her back feet and tail showed on the other. She basked in the cascade of golden hair across her body.

She'd decided she didn't want scales any longer, and had changed her skin to a soft, downy fur. Goonthur seemed to like it, because she felt the warrior relax under her gentle, rippling caresses.

The wizard glowed in her vision. The innate magic he suppressed mingled with the swirls of his fears and confidence issues. But he smelled like onions, sweet musk, and cider—which was an okay combination of smells—but she preferred the tangy smell of testosterone and sweat from her man. It was so much more…manly.

The boy-child, Manx, was barely a hatchling. He was a vortex of indecision and self-righteous confusion. She could see the creature's internal struggle—wanting to prove himself to the others and wanting to not care what they thought—and it made her roll her ethereal eyes.

Stupid humans, always so worried about what all the other humans thought about them. But it was the ones that cared the least who drew in the most others to do things for them. It was a weird dichotomy of people.

The dragon wondered if the people knew about the hundreds of spiders lurking in the corners, recesses, and shadows. Dozens of the arachnids had watched Mogits's hand reach under the bed, sliding a few centimeters below their bulbous bodies. Dozens more watched from each of the wardrobes, hidden in the folds of clothing. The mage had even put a few in his backpack with the pouches of coins.

Goonthur was vibrating. He was talking, and it always made his whole-body rumble. He sounded upset, and Blueberry sat up, and grabbed the man's ear to pull herself upright. Stroking the man's temple with a clawed hand, she soothed him.

The tension melted from his taut muscles, and his jaw relaxed. *Poor Goonthur,* she thought, *he just wants friends. His father and family put too much pressure on him to be what they expected instead of what he is.*

She knew what she wanted; to let this man's inner greatness shine out. Of course, that meant straightening him out on a few things. He needed to quit trying to control everyone and everything.

I'll start working on that right now, she thought, *starting with him mansplaining all the things to Rose. She's a good priestess and will be better for him if he just lets her be who she is. Funny, that he'd try to do the exact same thing to everyone else that his family did to him. But humans are dumb that way and give out what they know!*

Luna Rose rose to her full height, stepping into the bullheaded man's personal space, her nose a hand-span from his.

"You will not push me around!" She punctuated each angry word by jabbing him in the chest with a finger.

The big man winced, raising a hand to the side of his head, and looking at his shoulder.

Luna tensed, unsure if he was going to hit her or not. She'd pushed for it, figuring if she whipped him in a fight, he'd show a bit more respect, but she wasn't looking forward to a physical confrontation.

"Ow!" Goonthur pulled away from the priestess. "She bit me!"

"No, I didn't!" Luna stepped back, her face twisting with confusion and offense.

"I didn't see her do anything," Manx mumbled.

"Not Rose," the barbarian shook his head, then pointed at his shoulder, "her!"

"Nothing's there, big guy." Mogits smiled his secret smile he so often used. His voice carried a tinge of humor mixed with the suggestion of trouble. "Who, exactly, are you seeing over your shoulder that bit you?"

Goonthur heaved a sigh that was heavy with exasperation. "Blueberry!" He jutted his finger at the empty air beside his head. "I know she's small, but you must be able to see her."

"Um…" the priestess traded a concerned look with the thief and wizard.

"Yeah!" Mogits nodded vigorously. "We see her, champ! Don't we, guys?" The mage slapped the big man on the bicep, receiving a glare for the overly familiar gesture.

The other two nodded slowly, their faces dubious.

"Oops, almost clipped her there! Her foot was hanging down. Sorry about that!" Mogits smiled a big grin.

"She's a dragon. She doesn't have feet. She has claws. How could you even call them feet? Are you even looking at her?" Goonthur put his hands on his hips, then dropped them self-consciously.

"Of course we can!" The wizard reassured the man. "Slip of the tongue. I was so excited to see a real-life dragon

61

I got a bit tongue-tied, that's all. Shall we head upstairs?"

"Good idea," Luna agreed, "let's keep moving. We all see the…dragon. Let's move on."

"After you two," Mogits gestured towards the stairs, indicating the barbarian should lead the way.

The wizard moved to the sconce where he'd set his torch, recovering it from where he'd left it.

The big guy turned with a dissatisfied grunt and headed up. Luna followed him, morning star in hand. Manx went next, with Mogits taking up the rear.

"New shoes?" Manx asked over his shoulder.

"These old things?" Mogits asked. "They're just something I threw on."

As the group ascended, the mage lit the sconces along the steps, like he had on the last flight of stairs.

They heard and smelled the next room before they saw it. The sound of bubbling liquids and crackling flames filled their senses once they reached the landing.

Light spilled through splits in broken shutters that covered windows, evenly spaced along the walls. Cracked windows were coated with soot and grease, causing the sunbeams to smear yellowish color as they washed across the contents of the room.

Scattered throughout stood dozens of unaligned tables, and bookshelves lined the walls from floor to ceiling. Books, decanters, trinkets, knick-knacks, bric-à-brac, and tchotchkes lined the wooden shelves. On the tables were beakers, tubes, and jars—with burners under many of them.

Spiders with glowing abdomens skittered along the corners of the walls and along the rafters. A thin wisp of vapor wound through the rafters and curled around chandeliers that held dozens of candle stubs each.

The ever-shifting light from the creatures, combined with the jets of flame of the burners from below and the flickering candle stubs from above, revealed a rod-iron, circular staircase spiraling upward on the far side of the magical laboratory.

"That probably leads up to the cupola," Mogits pointed at the steps.

"Cupolas are rounded and have walls. I thought it was more of a gazebo," Manx shrugged, "but those tend to be in gardens and stuff."

"Pagoda, maybe?" The wizard suggested.

"No," Manx sneered, "those are like covered railings overhead. This one was more enclosed. I could agree to it being a rotunda."

"Aren't those more of a freestanding thing? Kiosk, perhaps?"

"Will you two shut it?" Luna growled. "We're not alone in here."

The priestess pointed at an upright crate on the far side of the room. The others squinted into the gloom at the box.

"It has a face!" Goonthur said with disgust.

"And arms! Sorta?" Mogits exclaimed. "Is that an eggbeater? And a…plunger?"

The box slowly pivoted towards them.

It was a weatherworn brown of aged wood, with iron straps bolted to its octagonal shape, holding it together. Wider at the bottom than the top, it tapered upward and a metal dome topped it, which in turn had a weather vane and lightning rod shaped like a dancing wyvern on top. Inside the curved topping was a pale, bloated face that grimaced at them.

"That's more of a cupola," Manx pointed at the top of the moving crate.

"Yeah, I can see that now that you said it," Mogits agreed.

"You killed the princess," said a broken voice from within the shell of the device across the room.

"Well, we didn't mean to," Mogits said, his tone friendly, "but she wouldn't quit singing…and we're not critics or anything, but it was literally killing us."

"The children won't have a mother now," the box squawked, its voice jittering with each syllable. "You must pay for that murder!'"

A spatter of horrific rain began to fall. Dark forms—from the size of coins to the size of dinner plates—dropped from the ceiling, landing around and on the adventurers. A torrent of arachnids gushed from the dark corners and recesses, geysers of the spindly forms erupted from pitchers and vases, and a flood of them rolled in a wave from underneath the tables and shelves around the room. The creatures skittered and scurried up the bodies of the four—small legs as fine as hairs tickling across the flesh of the groups' arms, necks, and any other exposed flesh.

The room flashed a bright white, then everything faded to black.

Luna woke. Blinking, she opened her eyes. A bright flash of pain shot from through her neck, which had fallen so her chin rested on her chest. Her head felt like it was stuffed full of feathers, and her mouth felt like she'd been eating them.

Lifting her head, she rolled her neck in a circle, trying to loosen the knots. Cartlidge popped and crackled as she tried to focus her blurred vision. Her hair caught on something sticky, and she jerked forward, feeling strands pull free from her head and whatever it was behind her.

Her arms were numb and secured above her. They tingled and bit at her awareness. Squinting, Luna looked up. Hands covered in webs, she felt the tickle of movement along her fingers and spiders the size of her palm moved across her wrists, spinnerets spewing out grey threads and thickening the silk bonds already there. She didn't see or feel any wounds, but she was groggy. Either magic or venom, she guessed.

Taking stock, she looked herself over. She still had her armor, but her pack and weapons lay nearby, the leather straps cut, or chewed through. From the light coming in, she decided that the sun was setting.

Strung up to her right was Manx. Mogits and Goonthur hung to her left. None of them looked any better or worse than her.

"Daughter," the jittery voice screeched, the same voice she'd heard from the crate earlier, "you are awake. I am preparing your transformation. You shall take the place of the princess, though you will never hold the position of honor she did."

"I don't think so," Luna growled through gritted teeth.

The warrior priestess pulled at one hand with all her strength. The threads holding her moved, but barely.

She had no leverage. Twisting her legs, she tried to push them backwards, to find the wall, to gain some footing to break free. Bound—webbing covering her from ankle to hip—she couldn't move more than twitching.

She went limp, panting.

"You will not break free," the voice said, the tapered box coming into view. "But I will release you once you've changed and dedicated to Mother and are ready to help fulfill her plan."

"I think he's gonna monologue," Mogits whispered.

Luna jerked to look at the man.

He still hung limply in the spider's prison, eyes closed and face drooping. One eye opened, looked at her, blinked once, then closed. She could barely make out his cynical and amused smile in the dim light.

"No, no, no. Listen," Mogits mumbled, barely moving his mouth, "it's a good thing. Get him talking. Any time you buy us will be a good thing. I still have a few tricks up my sleeve. Don't worry, trust me." He drew the last words out.

She'd heard that man use them before, many times. It usually ended with them being chased out of town in the middle of the night, or a tunnel collapsing that was the only way out of whatever cavern or dungeon they were raiding.

Out of the corner of her eye, she could see the crate guy floating into the circle of light around her and her companions.

"Fine then, Boxey," Luna snapped, turning to look at the face resting inside the dome, "I'll bite—perhaps a bad turn of phrase, given my circumstances—what's the big plan then?"

"Derek!" The voice rose in a shrill trill, grating on the woman's last nerve.

"What?" Luna spat. "Who's Derek?"

"I am Derek," the thing in front of her whined, "Lord of this keep, and master of the denizens within. I am the one mage who can talk to the children, who commands them, and who they adore and serve."

"So, this is your place?" Luna asked. "You should've had them capture a maid or housekeeper from the village. This place has more cobwebs than is healthy."

"Do not mock me, woman!" Derek screeched. "You do not crave my wrath!"

"Oh wow, I didn't know anyone actually talks that way," Mogits muttered. "Nefarious."

"What?" Luna said to the wizard through the side of her mouth.

"Ask him about his nefarious scheme." Mogits slowly whispered. "Make sure you use the word nefarious."

"Okay, fine," Luna sighed. "Oh my, oh my, whatever is your nefarious plan?"

"Scheme," Mogits hissed.

"Scheme, alright?" Luna snapped. "What is your nefarious scheme?"

"Yes, daughter," her captor seemed pleased, "that is a fine query. Extermination! I shall exterminate the humans, the same way they attempt to exterminate the children of Mother! For too long, man has thought he was the supreme hunter. The apex predator. The top of the food chain."

"That's rather sexist," Luna interrupted, "what about women? It's not just men who do all these things, we're just as horrible. Come on, I mean, this is the dark ages and all, but you seem like an enlightened villain. After all, you are all about the Mother. So, give credit where it's due."

Luna missed the next crazed words from the man because whispering from Mogits distracted her. When she turned to her companion, he was still feigning unconsciousness, but was having a quiet argument with someone or something. Luna looked around, trying to see who he was talking to, but she didn't see anyone.

She turned away from the madman beside her, and back to the madman in front of her.

"...and they have ruined the world, worse than any locust or parasite! Not like a true hunter, but like a wasteful plague that kills indiscriminately!" Derek was screeching. "Wouldn't you agree?"

"Oh, I can honestly say that every word I heard made perfect sense. Incredible how you put it though, dazzling rhetoric, interesting theories, and...yeah, it was good." Luna said.

She felt herself drop a few centimeters, but enough that she wanted to look up and check her bonds.

"Will I be freed soon?" The words slipped from her before she realized she had said them.

"Yes," Derek was in a frenzy now, the accoutrements attached to his wooden and iron casing waving wildly, "all shall be free soon! Free from the bonds of this earthly and mortal coil! And you shall help me free them as we come together with the children of the Mother and exterminate, exterminate, exterminate!"

"Stall him," Mogits whispered. "Get him to turn away, distract him."

"And how am I supposed to do that?" Luna said through gritted teeth.

"With the magics, I will transform you, just as the princess had been transformed. You will lead the armies on silent feet, and in the night, we shall kill all men, um, people...in their beds!" Derek replied, thinking the question had been for him.

"Oh, that's interesting..." the priestess's eyes darted

about the room, trying to figure out how to get the man to turn around, "…how will you do that? The magics, I mean. That must be very difficult or take some great and powerful artifact."

"I am a mighty mage and can manipulate the very fibers of the universe." The captor spun towards the tables behind him. "See these chemicals? I made them from the blood, bone, and hair of people. I have blended them with that of the children, learning the secrets of how to combine the two different creatures into one being of such power they will be unstoppable!"

Luna slipped another fifteen centimeters, her feet just a hand-span from the floor.

"You're going to make spider-men?" She pulled on her bonds and found that she could move her wrists further from the wall. "Can you do this with other races also? Maybe the green goblins, the hobgoblins, or even the rhinos of the southern plains?"

"What?" Derek paused in his rant. "Yes, yes! That would be perfect. This is why you will make the perfect vessel to replace the princess! Well, except for the rhinos. Can you imagine them with eight legs and mandibles? Ew, just creepy."

The entire floating crate shuddered as the man shivered at the thought.

"Chelicerae," Luna said reflexively.

"What?" Derek spun towards her again.

"Oh, dammit," she sputtered, stopping her struggles, "spiders have chelicerae, not mandibles. You should know that already if you're trying to turn people into spider-people."

"You know so much about the children," Derek's voice gushed with praise, "perhaps you may one day be princess. I once again must declare my brilliance at choosing you to become Mother's next disciple!"

Aretha, my goddess, give me power and strength and assist me in my moment of need. Luna Rose silently prayed, *Oh, and if you have a little more to give, maybe you could turn this idiot back around?*

The ranting man smoothly turned a small circle and hovered away in the other direction, still prattling on about his genius. The priestess gave thanks to her goddess, and memories of her training trickled into her thoughts.

She hadn't entered the convent willingly, but in her time there, she'd been one of the best and brightest acolytes in the place. She excelled in a few areas. Well, two areas. Combat and the healing arts.

She was particularly good at bashing people with heavy, blunt things. She had a natural talent for the arcs of the weapons and finding the points where they'd do the most damage.

A close second was knowing how to fix the people she, or others, broke. She could set a broken bone in minutes, pick out the right combination of herbs to mix for a fever, and—the one thing she was praised most for, and she liked the least—call upon her goddess to mend flesh and bone, and banish disease and sickness.

Her mind and attention snapped back to the present as her wrists began to tear free. Looking up, she watched the sticky strands of her bonds sever. A faint glow of blue shimmered between her hands, causing her to blink.

"A dragon?" Luna whispered.

She dropped to the ground in a crouch, webbing tearing away from her armor and body.

Glancing up at Mogits, he smiled and winked at her.

"Ala peanut butter and jelly sammiches!" The wizard shouted, and a ball of flame appeared above his hand.

The fibers of iridescent white around his forearms melted away under the burst of heat. Dark forms scattered, fleeing the mini-inferno. The man flipped forward; his feet still caught in the webbing.

The ball of fire flew from his hand, sailing through the air in slow motion to Luna's eyes. It landed, light as a feather, in the center of the table littered with chemicals. Rolling in a slow fiery amble down the middle of the wooden planks, small tendrils of flame reaching out and tickling things as it passed. The burners under beakers and bottles leaned towards their free-roaming cousin, flickering in eagerness to join the one-ball-parade. Apparatus shook and shimmied.

Derek, distracted by his own monologue, didn't notice the magical sphere calling to its captive compatriots.

With a clatter of toppling tubes and a clittering crash of glass, the burners freed themselves from the laboratory bonds that kept them from freedom. Chemicals released by the exodus of elemental revolution, spilled and spread across the surface of the flat wooden planks.

The table erupted into a pillar of flame.

7. Say the Magic Word...Say It!

Mogits threw his arms up to protect his face from the fall. The ball of fire touched his hair, and a wave of intense heat ran back along his head. The smell of singed hair and the crackle of crisping skin filled his senses.

Flinging the flaming orb away, he crashed to the floor, face first, and felt his nose pop. His feet were still entangled in the sticky mess along the wall.

Rolling onto his back, he looked up at the others. Manx was awake and twitching as the eight-legged jailers clambered across his face and body to get away from the expanding melt of flames and webs.

Blueberry was at Goonthur's wrists, gnawing away at his bonds to free him, just as she'd done for Luna.

Mogits had been able to see the dragon since entering the Inn. But the wizard noticed that few others could. Goonthur did, but Manx and Luna didn't. He just figured it was something to do with magical aptitude; he had it, and the others didn't.

The conjured creature was hardheaded though and definitely had a mind of her own, something Mogits hadn't encountered in a summoned energy. He found it fascinating and wondered how many times that had happened before. He had a vague idea where the gnome's—Darome—skill levels were, but a spell like this should be way beyond the man's ability.

It may have been the magic of the Inn, though. Mogits noted the oddities of the building. The shifting and changing doors that appeared in a haze then dissipated like a morning fog. And the people within spoke volumes of the magical magnetism of the place. The wizard had seen the dragon-blooded standing at the top of the stairs when he'd entered; the guy was a legend, literally. Grenedal had gone toe to toe—physically and mentally—with necromancers, demons, and other other-worldly beings. The man was a caster also, but dealing in other sorts of magics than what Mogits dabbled in.

The wizard lay on his back, staring at the ceiling and wondering if Hue Blueaxe—a longtime friend and companion of Grenedal—ever came to the Inn. That was when he noticed the flames licking the rafters.

Tilting his head further back and lifting his shoulders from the wooden planks of the floor, Mogits's world turned upside down.

The table where the flaming orb had landed was a sheet of fire, with a column or orangey-yellow dancing atop the surface like the element wanted a pole and a stage to do its art.

Mogits smiled at the thought of a curvy, sexy, elemental made of...

The man sat bolt upright, spinning where he sat to look at the inferno. The danger had already spread along the rafters, the webbing and sizzling and popping forms of the spiders feeding its frenzy. Now, it was beginning to waterfall—an oxymoron if Mogits had ever heard one—over the side of the table and onto the wooden planks of the floor. It was like watching the lovechild of a mysterious fog and an excitable grease fire take its first steps.

Leaping to his feet, the wizard called upon his magical knowledge, summoning every bit of wisdom and learning he'd collected in his time working with the arcane arts, and...nothing.

Yeah, he had nothing that would help.

A sudden yell made Mogits jump. Luna, in all her warrior-maiden glory, was hefting a stout leg of a table—that she'd apparently broken off with her bare hands—and shouting her battle cry as she charged the man in the box.

Manx, freed from his bonds, dropped to the floor. The gang member turned master thief was in a crouch, one hand splayed on the floor between his widespread knees, the other held out and slightly behind him for balance. The rogue surveyed the scene through a squint and a scowl, his usually bored and pouting expression forgotten.

He actually looks...interested, Mogits thought, *Moist Manx looks all intense and engaged. I've never seen him like this.*

The kid's hands twitched, and thin-bladed stilettos flashed in his grip. Manx looked to one side, then the other, his head moving the slightest bit. Then he melted into the dancing shadows caused by the flames, disappearing from Mogits's sight.

A loud thump from the wizard's other side drew his attention. Goonthur lay on the floor, moaning and rolling onto his back. Blueberry cooed and rubbed her snout against the barbarian's jawline.

The flames continued to flare away from where Mogits had hung only moments before, like the iris of some angry god...or Mother. Tightly wrapped cocoons appeared in the shadows, vaguely humanoid shaped, though they resembled bound coffins more than actual people. Green, magical threads of silk extended from the top of these bundles, and the wizard could see the throbs of magical energy pulsating outward. It was like watching a visual representation of a heartbeat. Each rhythmic pounding pushing the energy to...to where?

Mogits lifted his head, following the strands of arcane

conduits, trying to trace where they led to, and for what purpose. They were also as fire resistant as the cocoons, enchanted with the power of something more than just spider butts.

The lines led to beams on the walls, and they glowed in a deeper, pulsing light. They throbbed, the energy coursing to the center of the room, towards Derek.

Mogits looked at the master of the tower. The mage in a box was spinning in circles around Luna Rose, who was bashing madly at the foe. The woman was in full rage, her eyes wild, foam frothing from her lips as she screamed out unintelligible threats.

In the shadowed recesses on the other side of the room, Mogits saw Manx moving through the dim dancing haze of smoke and light. The thief was killing spiders with every movement, but there were hundreds of the things.

Just a couple meters from the wizard, Goonthur sat up, dazedly blinking at the room with unfocused eyes.

"Okay," Mogits breathed out to calm himself, "it's time to pull myself together and then pull them together. First things first, let's get the big guy on his feet and pointed in a direction where he can do either the most help, or at least the most damage."

The wizard moved to the barbarian's side, glancing at the ethereal dragon trying to cuddle the warrior.

"Goonthur!" Mogits grabbed the big guy by the crisscrossed leather straps of his empty sword scabbards and pulled their faces together. "You gotta get up! You were right, and we need you to do it, right now!"

"Wha-?" the barbarian muttered. "Do what?"

"You're right, it's the best plan. You gotta get our stuff from the corner over there…" Mogits grabbed Goonthur's chin and turned the man's head to look towards the pile of their gear that had been discarded to one side "…and I'll do some magic stuff or something. Brilliant plan. I couldn't have come up with a better one myself, no matter how I tried. You're the boss, and a genius!"

"Um, okay." Goonthur grunted.

"Now, get up…" the wizard strained to pull the big man to his feet, "…and Blueberry, you help guide him and make sure he doesn't get eaten by…you know, those things he doesn't like."

The dragon hissed, twisting her neck towards the wizard for a moment. Turning back to her beloved human, she stood on the man's shoulders and grabbed twin tufts of hair, ready to steer her favored steed into action.

"Is it spiders?" the barbarian asked. "I hate spiders. They make my tummy upset."

"Nope," Mogits patted the man on the shoulder, giving him a push in the right direction, "definitely not those. You got this! Go get em!"

The wizard watched the man totter away, like a giant, buff baby, toddling towards something shiny.

"One down, who's next?"

Luna wielded a table leg in one hand, and a twisted brass candelabra in the other, bashing at Derek in a dazzling display of…bashery. Green sparks flew from an unseen dome protecting the enemy. The ineffectiveness of the attacks enraged the warrior priestess even more.

"Well, she's keeping him busy," Mogits muttered. "Now, where's that kid?"

A glance around the chamber showed Manx walking along a wooden plank that encircled the room at four meters off the floor, slashing at the inhabitants in a flurry.

"Okay, time to redirect him." The wizard raised his voice. "Manx! The columns! Look for a thick cord of webbing. Cut it! That's what's delivering the villagers-in-the-cocoon's life forces to the bastard controlling the spiders. Severing that will be like severing his lifeline!"

The thief nodded the smallest nod and turned his attention from what he was doing. He leapt across the open air from the wall to the supporting column three meters away. The kid landed nimbly, like a cat turned lumberjack, flinging himself from tree to tree to make the next cut.

"That's two," Mogits grinned, "three if you count the distraction tank in the center there. Now, how am I really going to finish this? Put out the flames? Oh my, they are spreading quickly. Thank goodness the wood here is pretty much petrified, or we'd all be dead already."

A section of floor near the center fell away. Tables, test tubes, and other equipment spilled into the void, and a column of green flame shot upward a moment later.

"Perhaps I spoke too soon." Mogits backed away from the collapsing floor, looking towards Luna.

The warrior priestess threw her makeshift weapons away, squatted and grabbed a small round table by the legs catty-corner to one another.

Standing up, the table held in front of her like a giant shield; she charged Derek.

Slamming into the wooden casing hovering above the ground, the massive box shifted backwards towards the newly opened hole.

"Here!" Goonthur shouted.

Mogits was shoved back a step as the barbarian pushed a bag into the wizard's arms. Goonthur continued running past the mage, heading for Manx. The dragon clung to the warrior's shoulder, glaring at Mogits.

"Moist, catch!" the barbarian shouted, throwing the thief's satchel towards where the young man sawed at tangled knots of spider silk.

Without looking up, Manx held out one hand, caught the strap of the bag, twisted his wrist and elbow up and back, the satchel settling over his head and around his body.

The northern warrior made a ninety-degree right turn and headed for Luna, his duffel and her backpack each over a shoulder, his enormous sword slapping his buttocks in its leather scabbard.

Goonthur snatched up a long, thin table and held it in front of him like a spearman's body shield, charging towards the master of the tower.

Upon contact, a burst of white light flared, followed by

a noise that shook the stones of the building and sounded like a hundred giants clapping in unison.

The only time a noise like that had been heard before was during a historic meeting of the giant clans of the north, just a few days' walk from where Goonthur's tribe winters.

The opening speaker started with a joke on this very rare, and solemn moot and was met with that singular response. Instead of laughing, slapping weapons to shields, cheering, booing, or making any other noise…every single giant clapped once, and all at the same time.

Skalds tell that trees still don't grow in that grotto out of fear of another clap-occurrence, and even rocks avoid the place unless they have a thick coat of moss to protect them. To this day, northern barbarians never open a meeting with a joke.

Goonthur's people still speak of the day all the trees shed their leaves with a single shudder, and how the reindeer learned to avoid that entire region. As a side note, the Frost-Bitten Barbarian Clan changed their winter home, and now young warriors are tested by sending them to the place of the Giants' Thunder Moot and required to recover a single twig that is still shivering in fear of that day.

The adventurers, spiders, tables, and all the other things in the tower were thrown backwards against the outer wall, from the noise and the subsequent sound wave.

"He's still getting power," Mogits muttered from the corner he'd landed in. "We're not going to make it if this keeps up. I need to…reverse the polarity. Naw, just make it go from suck to blow!"

Mogits spun in a circle, looking for a way to do what he'd just described.

"But…how? How do I make the magic he's drawing on, the life force of dozens of villagers that have already been drawn into him, reverse and blow out his power? And will it kill us?" Mogits asked the smokey air around him.

"Awww, whatever." The wizard shrugged and began chanting. "Abracadabra!"

Pulling on the arcane energies, he drew the magic he could see into himself.

On one hand, it might give him all the power the enemy had drawn into himself, and he could use it to do amazing things. On the other hand, it might burn him out, turning him into a charred husk of magical residue.

The wizard watched the poor, dumb warriors charge the guy again, tables at the ready to push Derek back and over the precipice into the green torrent of energy guttering upward from the floor below.

He did have the thought that he was happy he'd looted the room below before he did this.

"Loot…" he groaned, "I haven't checked the shelves here for magical items and books!"

The process had already begun, but Mogits scanned the room in desperation, his natural greed fighting the oddly foreign impulse to save everyone.

To the east, a wand on a stand glowed with power. In the south, a small device wavered with enchantment of sound. And scattered around the room, fifteen books shimmered with an energy that showed that they might, possibly, probably, contain spells he could learn.

A slow surge built within him, a special, specific tickle that reminded him of that one time, his first time, with a woman. She had charged him for the wave of overpowering, and delightful pleasure she'd given him, and the rupturing pulse of magnificent ecstasy he'd felt that night. But this was on a different level. He felt it from his soul to his toes, to a tingle in his head. His vision cleared and sharpened, so exquisite and different from that moment of juvenile delight. Instead of overwhelming him, it focused everything.

So much power, he thought

He pulled, reaching out with his hands to lend motion to intent.

"Alakazam!" the wizard exclaimed, holding out his hands to receive his prizes.

The wand snapped to his waiting palm, covering the

distance of the room in a second. The small listening device flew to his other hand. Then the books came towards him. His heightened awareness showed the more than a dozen tomes gliding across the space. They were huge and heavy, and then they hit him. All at once.

He went sprawling.

Sitting up and taking stock, he saw the warrior and priestess hit the enemy caster, and the box-of-a-man slid backwards towards the hole. His plunger and overgrown eggbeater whirled ineffectively in the air as he was pushed backwards, teetering on the edge of the precipice.

Mogits pushed the energy away from him, feeding the extra towards the imprisoned silk tombs of the villagers. Energy danced along the silk bonds, washing over and soaking into them. The casings around the villagers split. People rained down, falling to their knees, faces, and in general slumping to the ground. But they were moving and probably breathing.

He'd done it.

The entire room erupted in magical, green flames. It didn't burn. Instead, it pulsed with power, alternatively drawing from the people and filling them.

Everyone swooned. Except Derek, who slowly slid backwards—accoutrements flailing—into the pit behind him. Then he dropped from sight.

A gout of verdant power burst upward, and the ceiling shattered, sending stones into the dusk sky. Which wasn't the problem—in fact, it was kinda cool—it was when the building blocks of the tower started coming back down that Mogits saw how it might be bad.

"To the spiral staircase!" Mogits panted.

The wizard scrambled, snatching up the wand and small swirly device that hit his hands moments ago and shoved them into his backpack.

The flames devoured everything as many of the villagers pushed to their feet and staggered towards the rod-iron stairs that spiraled upward to the roof and...cupola?

Gazebo? That little bump of a building on the roof.

Manx leapt through the flames like a specter of death, soot and webbing trailing from him in streamers. He pushed and herded the townsfolk towards the only exit available.

The mighty Goonthur (Mogits hesitated as he realized how heroic the man looked) lifted three people and carried them towards the aperture that might mean escape and living. The dragon darted ahead, leading the way for her human.

Luna called upon the power of her goddess and the devouring flames of magic bent away from her as she shepherded a half-dozen people towards the steps. When the woman reached the metal stairs, she uttered more words and the purifying waters of her goddess burst from thin air to douse the glowing metals steps. The metal warped and bent, but the people could put their feet on them and start the climb to the fresh night air, and potential freedom.

"Freedom?" Mogits coughed. "Aw, how're we going to get off the roof? Maybe we can climb down, or use a rope, or something?"

The wizard pushed to his feet, his backpack bulging with books. He'd only gotten less than a half dozen into his pack, but he thought they were the good ones.

The idea of losing knowledge made him queasy. Not because of civilization and recovering horded magics lost through the greed of others—no, not ever that, this was about him, really it was—but because he wanted an easier life. The arcane formulas and power within these books could mean he could retire and maybe even buy a little inn of his own. Then he could just charge people to help them, making a comfortable living through other people's laziness and hope.

He darted for the stairs, weaving between bursts of flame and scurrying spiders. He reached the steps last, looking back to seeing the few people who didn't make it, writhing in the torrent of fire.

"I don't care, they don't matter," Mogits choked, not

from emotion, but from the smoke, he told himself. "At least I survive, they don't matter. I don't care."

He put a foot on the spiraling metal and turned away from the people screaming behind him. Then he moved onward.

The explosion from below threw the mage up, his body tumbling along the underside of the stairs before being launched into the waiting night sky.

Gravity called for its due, and he fell back down and hit the outer circle of the parapet of the rooftop. The center of the tower exploded and stones the size of loaves of bread fell towards the helpless mage.

Travis I. Sivart

8. Flailing to Launch

Luna pushed the people on the roof into the small room on top of the tower, making space for Manx as he guided more people into the already crowded area. Goonthur burst onto the rooftop, three small children in his arms.

"Maybe you aren't all ego," the priestess muttered, waving the big man past her.

The barbarian stared at her, confused. Goonthur, lost and in a daze, was following his feet without thought, and probably hadn't even heard the words. The tiny blue dragon hovered to one side, her head pivoting as she guarded him.

Moments passed, and then a last person emerged from the billowing smoke, Mogits. The man flew upward, a gout of flame following his flopping, flying figure.

The rooftop behind the priestess wobbled, a sharp cracking noise drawing her attention. She turned to see the stones rippling like the surface of a lake, then erupting upward in a geyser of rock. The priestess watched the smaller components of the roof go up, and the mage come down.

He hit the ground, landing on a giant bulging bag

strapped to his back.

"You looted the damn place?" Luna growled, eyeing his backpack. "People were dying, and you took the time to grab things to sell? You're filth, you greedy bastard."

Mogits didn't respond, his gaze darting between the objects on the landing. Standing, he wheezed and panted, stifling a coughing fit.

"Did you even hear me?" The woman warrior curled her hand into a ball and drew it back.

The priestess's fist connected with the wizard's nose, and the man crumpled back to the ground.

"The ballista…" Mogits gagged.

Leaning to one side, he spat a glob of thick, grey phlegm mixed with the blood that wound its way across his upper lip and pooled in the corners of his mouth.

The mage lunged forward, his hand sliding along a sleek emerald and polished silver stand that supported a magical globe.

His mind shifted from the world he knew to somewhere else. It danced along razor thin wires of perception and reality as it left his body behind. Mogits was on the furthest edge of a spider's web that didn't exist in his world, but was more real in this magical reality he'd entered when he'd touched the sphere on the pedestal.

Something pulsed at the center, a slither of a whisper sliding along his awareness. His ethereal feet moved of their own accord, drawing him down the wide funnel, and deeper into the electric blue of the energy arcing through the air. That same energy created the webs on which Mogits stood.

With that realization, the mage pulled himself to a stop. He struggled against the automatic moving of his non-corporeal limbs that were urged to answer a silent siren song of something in the center of this vortex.

Mogits jittered backwards. Falling, he caught himself

on his hands and crab-walked backwards. The image of a spider trying to escape from a child—after that child had pulled off four of its legs—came to mind.

Vibrations caught the man's attention, and the language of the pulses tickled at his perception. He hesitated, trying to figure out if he'd actually understood it.

It couldn't be that easy, could it? Mogits thought, meaning to say it out loud. *There's something here, something dark and foreign, lurking in the center of an event horizon that could catapult dozens of worlds, and even a handful of realities, into chaos and threaten to annihilate them.*

The hunger and the urge to devour those within reach washed over the mage. The desire to purge the universe of the weaker and lesser beings overcame the man.

Launch the attack, was the urge inside of Mogits, *feed the Queen, and conquer the realms.*

The wizard ripped a thread from the web of lies, deceit, and energy under his hands, the surrounding area collapsing and unraveling. Information flooded into his mind, filling it with the secrets of the world he lived in. Bleed-over from other realities pushed at his perception, and the larger picture washed over him.

So much opportunity.

He tore himself from that tangled web and launched his mind back into his physical body.

"Put the kid—Manx—on it," the wizard coughed, "and fire it."

The priestess hesitated, looking from the device in the round room to the mage.

The small building was open to the night, a short fence lining its perimeter. A huge crossbow-like contraption sat in the center. It was large enough for a man to lie on it.

"It's magical, and that crystal ball," Mogits continued, pointing at an orb swirling with lightning and blue mists, "controls it. And it's aimed towards Salami. It'll send people there, I swear. I've double checked this personally. The tower is burning. It's the only way."

Luna watched the man fall to the ground, hacking.

"To hell with you, wizard," she spat, "but I will do as you say, but you go last. And I hope to Aretha that you burn."

The authority in the tone the priestess used offered no room for argument, and Manx climbed aboard. Mogits lurched to his feet, still lugging his overfilled pack, and slapped one hand on the war machine, and the other on the glass sphere.

The mage muttered a word and Manx shot into the night, a scream of surprise echoing into the darkness.

"Goonthur, get on," Mogits croaked.

The barbarian didn't question the wizard for once, and climbed on, Blueberry flitting around the man in concern.

With another muttered magical phrase in a language long hidden from the world, the northern warrior shot into the night. The dragon launched herself after Goonthur, disappearing into the distance.

"Luna?" Mogits looked at the priestess.

"I will go, traitorous mage, but..." the warrior woman reached down and tore the backpack from the arcane trickster. "I will take this, and keep it, until you prove to me you can be trusted."

She punched him in the face one more time. He jerked backwards, his hands flying to his thrice shattered nose.

Climbing on top of the war machine, she held up her middle finger to the mage. The wizard looked at her, the thought of launching her across the woods towards the unexplored areas entering his realm of consideration.

But then again, he would've done something pretty close to what she'd done if their positions had been reversed, and he had any muscle tone and upper body strength.

He slapped the ball of glass, and the woman launched

into the night sky. The flail in her hand—an artifact she'd recovered somewhere below after savaging the lord of the manor with table legs—smashing the orb of power. A trailing scream followed her trajectory as it wobbled away from the tower.

The orb crackled and a sphere of energy burst from it, catching the villagers and tossing them over the side of the tower. Blue bubbles of magic surrounded them, and the wind tossed them in all directions. They floated away at the whim of air currents.

"At least they're safe." Mogits muttered. "Guess it didn't get me because I was anchored by the ballista, and the…"

He turned his head to stare at his only escape route. The globe was shattered, and pieces lay scattered across the stones at his feet. He stared at the magical conduit that would have launched him towards the town that had been threatened for months.

The top of the tower exploded again—causing Mogits to jump—widening the already sizeable hole in the center. Stones larger than a man's thigh burst into the sky. A sinister, shadowy shape rose from the burning depths below. The boxy form of the master of the house levitated into view of the trickster magician that had faked most of his career. Mogits watched as Derek—the mini-sauna-encased-caster of the arcane—came level with his line of sight.

"Oh, shit," the broken mage breathed, his body laying halfway across the war-weapon that no longer functioned because a priestess of respect broke the magical conduit of transportation.

Aretha may be a goddess of respect, but that wasn't terribly precise. The sisterhood of that specific religion often demanded certain mental and social caveats without backing it up with logic of why people should do those specific things. But Luna was specific. She wanted that respect due to her fighting prowess, her strength of will and personality, and never because she was charming or attractive.

"Fair enough," Mogits muttered, while shaking his head to the contrary, "but she should let herself be more than just respected…because humans are barely more than just dumb monkeys that jump up and down when something cool happens…something like her showing up."

The mage turned to look at his enemy and rival rising above the broken rock and mortar, wondering what he could do to defeat such an impressive foe. Then it came to him. The one way to make sure that a being of power would acknowledge and bow to someone of significantly less ability, and back down from a confrontation of ego…

"The Gods have spoken to me," Mogits intoned in a flamboyant and over-the-top tone, "and they have said that you and your matron have been found wanting and lacking. You are both less than they'd expected. You have failed, and that's why a rag-tag group of misfits who can't even relate or bond to one another…because of emotional and psychological issues…"

Mogits kept talking, the words and concepts growing larger with each syllable. He peppered the sentences with thees and thous, shan'ts and shalls. The being of immense power hovering, centered over of the hole in the tower hesitated. The mage on the ballista took advantage of this moment, casting the simplest of spells in his arsenal of words.

"Believe in me, because you can't handle your own issues," was the most basic of messages, but it had worked countless times throughout time and history. The flood of doubt from the man washed across Mogits, and Derek slumped in his makeshift coffin.

Mogits knew that he had no genuine power or ability. His magic lay in the mundane. In the simple ability of empathy and triggering others. He was a conduit, a catalyst, to the power from others. Maybe if he'd studied for the last few decades instead of running cons and scams, he'd be further along on that track.

The mage pulled in the emotional energy from his enemy. That tainted mix of uncertainty and power, the feeling of failure and doubt, filled him. He felt the power flow through him, a trickle of emotion and intent, growing as the enemy staggered under the weight of his own confidence issues. The elements answered his suggestion, rising to the beckoning of Mogits's minor talent. The trickle became a stream, and the stream became a river. The river changed to a torrent, and the magics caused the mage to stiffen in a rictus of sensation that bordered on pain. He felt weightless and realized the trees were spinning away below him.

He called upon the elements of fire and wind to pull the magical orb of power back into its original form.

Mogits's awareness expanded, seeing the orb that directed his path clatter to the stones, and roll into the burning hole at the center. The tower exploded behind him. The master, Derek, tilted in his casing, and plummeted into the inferno.

Spiders, seen as dots of reddish energy, darted from the area. Heading into the forest, the creatures—which ranged in size from a thumbnail to a horse—ran away from the tower, and toward Salami. Hordes of the creatures spilled from the shattered building, pushing out from the broken windows, underneath the foundation, and through cracks in the walls. The area was carpeted with thousands of the arachnids, legs moving in a hypnotic pattern, driven in the direction that the magic was focused.

He'd done as the Mother had commanded. Mogits had released the attack upon Salami. He'd failed in saving the village, and the magic urged him to follow the flow of energy to finish the job. The mage's magical awareness looked toward his—and the spiders below—destination, and he saw he was just slightly off course.

Luna landed, hitting the soft loam of a tilled field at the edge of the village. She rolled, the flail she still clutched slamming into the earth like an anchor. She lost her grip on the weapon, tumbling over again and again, before coming to rest on her back.

The sound of Goonthur's voice, shouting commands, came to her ears as she caught her breath. The barbarian was directing defenses to be constructed, and for people to arm themselves.

Tiggie's voice rose above the big man's instructions.

"Why the hell should we listen to you, you big dumb oaf?" The old woman's shrill question cut through the hubbub of other voices. "You're just a brute, and we don't think you have the sense that the gods gave to a drunken snail!"

The priestess sighed and sat up.

Manx stood to one side, picking at his fingernails, looking bored, as usual. The young man shifted and glared around him, eyeing the shadows of the buildings in the late afternoon sun with dual longing. He wanted to get out of the sun—understandable since he dressed in all black—and use them to disappear, his forte.

Bernie the blacksmith stood behind his grandmother with his arms crossed, glaring at the northern warrior.

Standing up, Luna dragged the flail from the fertile soil. Her first step staggered, but she pulled herself upright and her shoulders back with the next three steps. By the time she stood beside Goonthur, she was at what she thought of as her 'professional' posture.

People treated her differently depending on how she stood. When she was young, she'd hunch her shoulders and drop her chin, folding her hands in front of her. Oh, the other convent girls would tease and mock her without remorse. It didn't help that she'd been a broad-shouldered girl, with gangly limbs and knees and elbows that resembled knots in a cord. Even the sisters sneered at her, though Luna wasn't even sure if they knew they were doing it.

When combat training started, Luna's body changed. Part of that was the progression of puberty, but part of it was the sculpting process that came with daily exercise. The muscles on her legs and arms filled out, meeting with those large joints that had stuck out before. Melding into one limb, tone and strength showing in every movement, people had treated Luna differently than before.

But she'd been young, and without even knowing she did it, she'd pushed too far in the other direction. The girls who had once teased her received sound drubbings, and the sisters who had once scorned her received glares that could have made a horse climb a ladder.

During those years (or had it only been months, it was hard to tell), she'd walked around with her shoulders too far back, her chest leading the way everywhere she'd went. Her chin was too far up, causing her to look down on people. When she walked, she moved with her legs a little too far apart, and took strides that were a little too long. Every movement she made was a challenge to anyone in front of her.

And when she hunched her shoulders and brought her hands in front of her, well, it differed from how it had been before. Instead of looking meek and deflated, she now looked like she was about to sacrifice someone to some dark whim.

But she'd grown out of that phase and had practiced her stances. The meek one was rarely handy, but sometimes helped when dealing with someone who had an ego. While being defiant would lock them down, being humble made them give you their blessing. The psychopathic posture of shoulders forward, muscles rippling, chin dropped, and glaring up at someone through hooded eyes was handy when intimidating people with their impending and unavoidable beat down.

But, that middle ground of shoulders just slightly back, chin up just a little, and a calm but serious look on her face…that was the magical comfort zone that worked in almost every instance. It made people listen when she spoke, her confidence and poise making them give way without feeling like they had to. It was a posture of leadership without question, and people responded to it.

Luna stepped up to stand beside Goonthur, one hand on her hip, the other holding the meter-long handle with the flail, its spiked metal ball dragging behind her.

"We ain't gonna listen to you," Tiggie was griping, "you're nothing more than a blow hard that needs coddled for the sake of your own ego!"

"Listen, old woman," Goonthur growled, "you gotta get everyone to move the wagons and whatever else you got to this side of town, create a barricade to slow down the monsters that'll be coming this way."

"Did you see them coming?" Bernie huffed.

"No, but I…" Goonthur's voice rose in frustration.

"Then we have don't have anything to worry about!" Tiggie cut him off. "They've been there long enough, and we've been here even longer. I don't think they're going to change their habits now. They're animals, and they don't change what they do because you fell from the sky, yelling that it's falling."

"They are, and they are, and he's right." Luna interrupted the interrupter. "We've flown here using a magical launcher, and we blew up the master of the tower and his girlfriend. Didn't you see the explosion from here?"

"Well…yes," Tiggie said slowly, Bernie nodding behind her, "but we hoped that meant everything was dead. But if you say we need to get ready, then we will."

"And…" Luna went on, "you will listen to Goonthur about the defenses. He's from a powerful barbarian tribe that has done exactly this same thing—from both sides, defense and offense—many times. He knows how to set things up to give us the best chance to not just survive, but to win this."

"I do?" Goonthur gaped at Luna, the surprise of her

support throwing him off. "I do. I did. I mean, I have. I can help."

The big man tripped over the words, trying to recover.

"Great, Goonthur. You take over the village defenses, and I will organize people. Manx…" Luna looked around for the rogue.

The slim figure peeled himself from the shadows of the inn and sauntered towards her. He looked like he had bitten into a bad olive, his face sour, glaring around at the people like he'd rather be somewhere else.

Luna smiled at the lad as he walked up.

"Good," she said, "find the holes. Find the dark places, the shadows and gaps where these things will come in. Get some oil or traps laid down and be ready to set them off if we need to."

"They're spiders, though," Bernie grunted. "How can he know what they'll do? And do we really want this kid lighting our wagons and stuff on fire?"

"He is our spider specialist," Luna said, meeting the blacksmith's eyes. "He knows these creatures and what their weaknesses are, their tactics, and so on. If anyone can do it, he can. And it's better to lose some tables, chairs, and carts than to lose your lives. Isn't it?"

"Yeah," Manx sighed, "that's right. I need a team to help cover the things I set up."

"Great," Luna clapped her hands, "Bernie, you're with Goonthur. Tiggie, get Manx some people. Let's do this!"

"Great dearie," Tiggie linked her arm through Luna's, "and I'm with you. Us powerful women gotta stick together."

Travis I. Sivart

9. The Best Defense...

The next couple of hours were a flurry of activity ending in a bang. The first wagon to explode was on purpose, the other three were not.

The town had set to their tasks with enthusiasm, for the most part. Each of the adventurers had a half-dozen people following them around, taking commands, and distributing jobs to other villagers.

Whenever Luna suggested a change, Tiggie snapped and barked, making people jump to do whatever Luna said, even if it was merely an observation or passing mention. The town elder had the leatherworker following the priestess around, trying to size her for new protective pieces…just because she'd mentioned a rivet needed fixed on her steel and hide breastplate.

Manx led his group around, which comprised mostly street urchins, laze-abouts, and town drunks. They were all the sort of people who would run a scam, so they didn't have to get up from their chair, get a job, or ever have to do any kind of work at all.

But they listened to the street thief. He droned on,

huffing and sighing, about how it really sucked, but these things had to be done. His down-to-earth attitude, tired of dealing with everyone else's bullshit, made them feel the world-wise young man really got what they were going through on a daily basis.

What Manx suggested was interesting, the kinds of things that were worth getting off the couch to do. Things like blowing up the cart the wainwright used to take his goods to market while glaring at them as they leaned against the shady part of the pub or rocking in a chair on the porch of the general store. It would serve the bastard right, being all judgy and stuff. He didn't know them, didn't know what they went through.

Manx led a small parade through the town, pointing out which house had enough of a crawlspace to move through, but was small enough to hide under, or which roof could be climbed with ease using railings and posts, or which horse would panic whenever it heard anything resembling the crack of a whip, and that sort of thing.

Passing Goonthur's group, Manx sighed and shook his head—three younger men behind him imitated the move. The barbarian was doing everything wrong with the townsfolk. The big man talked like everything was some incredible skaldic tale from the northern wastelands and frozen tundra.

Is there any other sort of tundra? Manx wondered, his eyes still watching the barbarian passionately trying to convince the group of doubting men—led by Bernie—to bring out all the tables from the inn. And do spiders really live in the Ice Floe Straight beyond the northern wastelands? I understand that maybe some had grown thicker hairs—spines? Trichobothria? Setae? So many stupid names for hairs—and could insulate themselves from the snow and winds.

The thief refocused on Goonthur. Gesturing in wide circles, the barbarian was telling the townsfolk how to surround the core of the town, and how the spiders could climb or jump over things, but obstacles would still slow their approach. With each passing moment and word, the men around the big warrior looked a little more scared.

Manx sighed. "Come on," he gestured to the trio behind him, "and remember, stay behind me and don't talk. Your job is to be my intimidators, and your body language will do much more than any words. Nod, cross your arms, and look people directly in the eye. They hate that. If you're nervous, fiddle with one item; a toothpick, a coin, eat an apple, do anything except shift and shuffle. Messing with something makes you look relaxed and unconcerned, even when you're not."

The three men nodded, two of them crossing their arms. Each caught the movement of the other doing the same action, and both stopped, then uncrossed their arms. Seeing the other man had undone it, they both moved to do it again, watching one another.

Manx sighed and walked over to the barbarian and his group.

"Hey man," the thief whispered.

The villagers surrounding and complaining to the warrior—who was only trying to instruct them—quieted and looked at the newcomer.

"Manx," Goonthur huffed, "can't you see I'm busy? I don't have time to chat right now."

"Yeah, I know. You're always busy, big guy." The younger man murmured, and the crowd leaned in, like they were trying to hear a secret. "It's hard being such a powerful warrior that everyone always wants around. I saw how you killed all those spiders back in the tower. It was like you were born to do this."

The trio stood behind Manx, looking bored, but nodding. One had his arms crossed across his chest, the second was twirling a twig between his fingers, and the third was shifting his hands on his hips, trying to find the right stance to look cool.

"And I remember how you defended our camp that

one time," the rogue continued, "from those flying tree monkeys. It was like you were reading their minds, knowing exactly how they were going to come in. Anyone who doesn't listen to you is a moron, and probably committing suicide."

Slapping the barbarian on his bicep, Manx moved away, followed by his flunkies.

The men around Goonthur stared at the warrior with newfound respect and awe.

"As I was trying to explain," Goonthur growled, glaring at the thief's retreating back, "what we need to do is…"

"No need to explain any more, sir," Bernie said quickly, interrupting the barbarian. "We got it. Come on, boys, let's get the wagons, barrels, and grain sacks. We got some defenses to set up. We'll all be heroes if we do what Goonthur says."

"And our loved ones may survive," Malcolm—the whiney guy who'd been there when Goonthur first came to town—added, "that's good, too."

"Yeah, that too. Of course, that too. It's important they survive." Bernie's voice drifted away as he led the other men to start the preparations.

"What happened to Mogits?" Manx asked, looking between Luna and Goonthur.

The three had gathered together after setting the people of Salami to task. They stood in a small huddle, watching the sun set in the west, comparing final notes on how to survive the night.

"He couldn't make it." Luna's voice was tense.

Her two friends couldn't tell if it was regret or anger.

"What happened?" Goonthur asked. "I was…a bit out of it when we departed the tower. I really only remember Blueberry telling me where to go."

The thief and priestess exchanged a worried look.

"Things got too heavy for him, literally and figuratively," Luna snapped. "That's why he gave me his bags of goodies that he'd pilfered while we were all helpless or busy doing the heavy lifting. AKA…killing."

"I can't say I'll miss him." Goonthur sighed. "He was a stupid man, who was always making others feel stupid, but he had his uses in a pinch."

"Like when he burned the webs?" Manx asked, and the other two nodded reluctantly. "And brought us out of the trance the spider lady had us under? Or convinced Luna to distract Derek while we were all still drugged from whatever that guy did to us?"

Luna's head snapped towards the thief, a scowl turning her lips and brow down.

"Not to mention figuring out how to use the transport bow on the roof," Goonthur added, getting another glare from Luna for his input.

"Fine! He was useful." Luna grudgingly admitted. "But he was a conman and robbed everyone blind. He took advantage of every opportunity to scam, steal, or swipe anything he thought was shiny. Goonthur, he undercut your authority as party leader every chance he could."

"That's true," Goonthur agreed, adding in a mutter, "but you do that, too."

"And Manx," Luna went on, ignoring the barbarian's last comment, "he…he…he always undercut your ideas with some idiotic idea of his own."

"He really didn't," Manx sighed, "but if that's what you need to tell yourself, we all process grief differently."

"It wasn't your fault," Goonthur put a hand on the priestess's arm, "I'm sure you did everything you could to save him."

Luna looked at the man's hand on her, then slowly raised her eyes to his face. Her look was dangerous.

Goonthur jerked his hand back.

"Doesn't matter," the priestess said, "he's not here,

and we have things to do."

All three nodded, each face showing different emotions. Luna, anger. Manx, doubt. Goonthur looked sad.

They turned away from their huddle, each heading towards their respective duties.

A few hours after sunset, the horn sounded. Bells clanged and banged. Voices shouted, and people ran to their places.

Manx leaned against the side of the inn, his 'men' lounging around him.

The group had grown to over twenty men and women. Children as young as seven tagged along, being put to work as runners for supplies and information, bringing the total number of people around Manx to over three dozen.

He hated it. He worked alone, and all these people looking to him for leadership grated on his style. The kids weren't surprising to him, and once Luna had assured the parents Manx wouldn't see action and that it kept the kids out from underfoot, the adults had sent their spawn to help the thin, shady guy who had the town drunks actually contributing.

Snapping his fingers, Manx gave the command for everyone to wake up and be at the ready. He'd told the surrounding people to spread out, nap if they could, and watch for the signal to cause chaos for the enemy.

This was odd for him, because the people around him were like spiders in that they were loners and rarely, if ever, worked in groups. But tonight, both those around him and the spiders would work with others.

The first of the enemy, enormous spiders the size of horses, leaped over the makeshift barricades. Their spindly limbs curled under them in the jump, landing in a splayed legged stance.

With a wave of his hand, Manx gave the command to

light the fuses. Flint and steel sparked, miniature stars dancing and jittering to land on the oil-soaked rags that led to the first wagon.

Blue flame woofed into existence and shimmied its way towards the blockade. It jogged up the rag rope to the flatbed of the cart and exploded.

Chunks of flaming wood shot in all directions, landing in a five-meter radius of the transport. Debris rained down onto two other wagons close to it.

That was when those two also exploded. Flaming detritus scattered across the area, and people ran in all directions.

Goonthur shouted at the men running away, demanding they return and hold fast. In moments, the barbarian stood alone except for Malcolm, Bernie, and Eric—the guy with the gurgle voice.

Manx sighed; someone had put a bit too much accelerant into the rags on the back of the wagon. Watching the series of smaller explosions, he noticed the group of children jumping up and down in excitement at the pyrotechnic display, slapping their hands together in a group high-five.

Then the kids started screaming, dancing and lifting their knees high. But it wasn't the celebratory kind of dance or screams. The thief looked down and saw the ground moving underfoot. It looked like a carpet had come alive, and he realized it was thousands of smaller spiders coursing past him and into the village.

One bite from a spider wasn't so bad for most folks; but a dozen bites, or a hundred, and even the healthiest person was likely to have a reaction.

Under Manx's advisement, they hadn't expected this to happen so early in the attack. He'd said the smaller spiders would take longer to get here.

Logic-ing it through, the rogue decided the smaller spiders must have ridden on the larger ones, allowing the expected waves to come all at once, in a single, massive, overwhelming attack. They'd prepared for this, but expected it to come later.

Luna shouted commands at the women, who pulled soaked blankets from rain barrels. They shook them in the air, fanning them out and dropping them on the ground.

The ladies danced across the material, stomping and crushing the miniature invaders. Others, bolder than the dancers, dropped to their knees with rolling pins, planks of wood, and anything else they could get their hands on. They smashed the creatures underneath, killing any that didn't smother from the wet blanket.

Mogits watched from the edge of the woods as the fireball shot into the sky, the wagons blazing in the night air.

The mage had landed, quite uncoordinated and embarrassingly, in a tree to one side of the village. He'd blacked out and woken—just before sunset—hanging precariously from one leg a few meters above the ground.

He wasn't wanted here, but this was his gig. He'd chosen it, convinced the others to go on it, and gathered the loot when they couldn't do anything more than stare at a dancing spider-lady. He'd burned the webs, defeated the boss, found their escape route, and saved the lives of his three companions and many of the lost villagers. He'd be damned if he would not be here for the climax of the story.

They might not respect him or even like him, but he'd earned his place in the group and wouldn't be tossed aside...no matter how they felt about him.

Torches on stakes, placed along the perimeter of the town, lit the night. Mogits crept forward to the edge of the glowing circle of light, and he took in the scene.

Goonthur stood in a circle of spiders, Blueberry perched on his shoulder. Damn, that man could swing a sword. The fast-moving spiders were eviscerated whenever they got close to him. The mage could see the look of disgust and fear on the man's face as he hacked and speared the enemy, but gave a brief nod of respect, as the barbarian did what needed to be done.

Luna was a frenzy of movement, her fit form gliding between the ladies of the village. Every woman around the priestess had faith they'd be protected as they dropped wet blankets over the smaller spiders, smothering and smashing them.

The priestess called upon the wrath of her goddess to empower her and protect the other women. She glowed—literally, a nimbus of light surrounding her—as she swung the flail in her hand. She crushed larger arachnids, spinning to kick another away, then swinging the ball and chain weapon to crush it in midair.

Manx was the hardest to spot. The youngest of their group appeared from a shadow, knives flying from his hands. He darted and spun through the enemies, recovering his blades, then disappeared into the smoky gloom around the village. Popping back into existence just beyond the next building, he'd slash a few hairy legs off a beast, then stab upward into the monster's thorax, felling it.

The thief disappeared again, and Mogits thought of the legendary 'Shadow Dancers' of the Lost Cities. Did this kid know the secrets of a clan of thieves and assassins who could move from one shadow to another, using a form of magic that the Great Collapse had devoured?

"How the hell do I help with this?" Mogits muttered aloud. "Or should I just go find the shit I picked up and head for the inn?"

He mulled it over, looking at the fight.

The villagers weren't doing as well as they thought though. They fought like people who had nothing to lose, because they'd already lost it all. And they had.

The wizard could see dozens of people slapping at their arms, legs, and bodies. The spider's venom coursing through them from a dozen, or a hundred, bites. Some already lay writhing on the ground, foaming at the mouth from the toxin. Others lay bloated and dying, their bodies swollen from the deadly bites.

"They're screwed!" Mogits spat. "I can't help them. The only answer is one of two things; wait until the spiders leave and get my stuff, or go in now and get out while they're all distracted. Spiders, villagers, and my...friends."

Looking down, the mage stared at his feet. He watched the curled toes of his purplish-pink shoes as they bobbed up and down in his indecision.

"Fine, I go in now, but I will not help them. They deserve whatever they get."

The mage ran forward, gritting his teeth and growling under his breath.

Growling? He thought. *Have I picked up some less than savory habits from Luna? Ew!*

He leaped at the building in front of him, turning sideways as the magic of the slippers kicked in. He fell to the side of the building, landing on his feet and standing upright. The world was turned sideways, the magic of the shoes shifting gravity so the mage could run along the wall like it was flat ground.

Mogits ran up, lifting a leg over the eave of the building—so his feet didn't both leave the surface of the structure—and his body swung up to the roof. Darting across the rooftop, he stopped at the far edge, looking at the chaos of the battle below.

"Presto change-o!" Mogits shouted.

The minor magics at his disposal heightened his senses and his sight, sense of smell, hearing, and touch grew to dynamic proportions. He looked in the direction of the tower and saw movement. As his vision clarified, he saw hundreds of spiders—the size of attack dogs—lurching towards the village. They didn't scurry like the others. Instead, they lunged. Thick forms that were solid and heavy lumbered towards the hamlet.

"Oh shit," Mogits muttered, "how many of them will

die when those get here? A better question is; how many will survive?"

Shaking his head, the mage reconsidered his course of action. What did it mean to him if a bunch of dumb hicks died? And what about Goonthur, Manx, and Luna?

"It would thrill Goonthur to die in battle, and I could live to tell his tale." Mogits murmured, his fingers moving through his pouches, searching for anything helpful. "Manx, well, I like the kid. I mean, he's a weirdo, but aren't we all? Well, worth keeping the freaks alive to mess with the muns. As for Luna, well, geesh. All she wants to do is help people. Does she deserve to die? Do any of them? Even dumb hicks deserve to be the hero of their own story."

Mogits hesitated.

He sighed, his shoulders slumping.

"I know what I should do," he sighed again, "I should get the hell out of here, and go live to drink another day. But, since when did I do what anyone ever expected of me?"

He straightened his shoulders, eyes narrowing as he focused on the battle below.

"But to be clear," he said, "at least to myself; I'm only doing this to get the reward, not because of anything else!"

He threw himself off the building and into the night, shouting one of the few magical phrases he knew.

Travis I. Sivart

10. Music Soothes the Savage Beast

"Bippity boppity boo!" Mogits shouted, landing upright and thrusting his hands out before him.

Manx turned at the sound and saw the mage drop to the ground, fire erupting in a stream in front of the wizard. Spiders burst into flame, curling and crackling as the moisture inside them turned to steam.

"That's...unexpected." The young man smiled. "But hell yeah, let's kill these bastards!"

The last words were uncharacteristically loud and shouted to the group of flagging miscreants that followed the thief into the battle.

The fight raged, most of the larger attackers laying in upside down heaps, legs tucked into their abdomens. The smaller attackers scattered, running for the cover of buildings and sheds.

Looking towards the edge of the light surrounding the town, Manx could taste victory. That was when dozens of spiders, each the size of a guard dog, skittered over the top, under, or around the smoldering defenses of the village.

"Gin-soo! Gin-soo!" yelled the mage, throwing blades

that glinted bright in the torchlight.

Wave after wave of spiders appeared. Hard-shelled, the monsters spat globs of webs from abdomens tucked under their bodies, raising their selves as high as they could go on spindly legs to shoot underneath.

Villagers stopped in their tracks as the viscous globs cemented them to the hard-packed earth.

A second wave leaped over the first, landing on people's shoulders and stabbing down with pincers.

The smaller ones that had been running for cover reversed their path and returned to the fight. The mass of mini marauders blanketed the citizens, dozens of bites thrusting toxin into terrified townsfolk.

Manx watched his people—*what? They, all of a sudden, are my people? Do I really feel some responsibility for these villagers?*—and his body locked up. Every muscle tightened, and he refused to be beaten. His mind spun, trying to find some way to overcome this horror. He wanted to escape into his music.

That idea tickled at his awareness, hinting at something more, something hidden behind the curtained folds of his awareness.

"My music!" He gasped.

The thief dug into the pouch on his hip, gaping at the rushing horde of monsters. He pulled out his small gramophone, the creatures only a few meters away.

Turning the dial and staring with wide-eyed horror at the tide of death rushing towards him, he found the one song that he so desperately wanted to hear at that moment. Cranking the handle of the music box, a tinny tune wailed. The Spider-Queen's voice rose over the battlefield.

The humans turned to look at him, freezing in place as the hypnotic song grew. They were stunned and immobilized, stuck in place just as he was back in the tower. That reaction guaranteed their death.

Goonthur's sword dropped from his loose fingers, falling to the ground beside him. The big man swayed gently, his head tilted to one side, watching Manx crank out the tune.

The priestess was in her throng of women, as they stood facing the thief, heads lifted to the night sky as if listening to something from far away call to them on the wind.

But Manx wasn't frozen. He could feel the movement of the music deep inside him. It was as if a spider web of melody was spreading outward from him and across the village and surrounding woods.

He could sense each creature in the web. Humans struggling against their unseen bonds, and spiders running along the threads as easily as a man runs down a road.

Reaching out, he locked down the movement of the spiders. The beasts stopped in place. Cutting the bonds around the people of Salami, he freed them from the call of the siren's song. They jerked back to awareness.

The fibers vibrated inside the young man, and he followed them deeper, seeking the middle. Something dark pulsed at the epicenter of Manx's awareness, and an answering song echoed from the dark pit within him. It felt ancient and knowledgeable, but not on an intellectual level, rather more on an instinctual one.

The onyx world within the thief expanded, and his awareness sought a point of reference to help get his bearings. His mind struggled, searching for something to latch on to. A pinpoint of light appeared in the distance. His awareness rushed towards the cold white dot, drawing near to it. The object shimmered, wavered, and then exploded in a shower of sparks on a horizontal plane. An arc of thousands of white-hot dots moved up and away from the source explosion, becoming small suns that shot into the endless black.

The stars expanded across the cosmos, filling the void of creation. In the middle of all that energy and worlds spinning away like they were trying to escape some predator. A light winked out. Then another, and another. Dozens of suns disappeared, drawn into something that was…very hungry.

A sound vibrated along the silken cord that led to the origin of the dark. It started as a whisper, then became a baritone thrum, though it held no masculinity or femininity.

Come to me, the command didn't come from a voice, but an impulse, *bring me nourishment. Feed me.*

Manx jerked away, repulsed by the intensity of the demand. He felt himself sliding towards the being in the center of the web. It felt reluctant, torn between taking him or using him as a tool to bring in more. So much more.

His awareness slammed back into his body, his hand still turning the crank on his music box. He watched his fingers shaking on the tiny, bent arm of the machine. Amplified, the tinny song coming from the device was so much more than it had been before he'd gone inside himself and to that place.

He looked across the killing field, his gorge rising as he thought about the slaughter in front of him, and what was to come.

The villagers were running through the invaders, bashing and slashing at the immobile attackers turned victims. Spiders collapsed, hacked in half, or crushed by barrels, staves, rakes, and wagons by terrified and desperate people. Anything the people of Salami could get their hands on went into the effort of crushing the alien invaders.

Goonthur's battle cry ripped through the night, cut by Luna's war shout. The two fought side by side, dancing the elegant steps of death that came with the experience of war and killing. It wasn't a brutal process, but more of a tedious and monotonous march towards an inevitable goal.

Mogits leaped in front of an older couple who were on fire duty—making sure the flames and explosions never reached the buildings—hewing down a spider with blade and flame.

The mage bounced forward, three small leaps covering a dozen meters. Landing beside a group of urchins, he flipped an enemy upside down and gutted the beast.

Scanning the field of carnage, Manx saw most of the attackers were dead, on fire, or being eviscerated. The call of the thing from beyond tickled at his thoughts, urging him to…

He tore his hand from the box, threw the device to the ground, and crushed it under his heel. The brass and wood box bent, then shattered under his foot.

Manx's head spun, and he wobbled on his feet, a wave of nausea rolling through him. He bent double and hurled. He continued to heave and choke, long after dispelling the contents of his belly.

"You okay, Moist?" A deep voice asked, and the young man felt a huge hand on his shoulder. "I mean Manx."

Looking up, the thief saw Luna and Goonthur standing over him, Mogits a few meters behind the two.

"Yeah," Manx sighed, "fine. So, stop touching me. Remember the no touching rule."

Goonthur jerked his hand back.

"Mogits," Manx croaked, waving the mage forward, "help me stand."

The wizard moved forward, taking a wide path around Luna, who glared at him.

Mogits slid an arm under Manx's, helping the younger man stand. The thief was pale and teetered on his feet.

"I saw you," Manx turned his head and spat some of the remaining vomit onto the ground, "saving people. Pretty selfless for such a me-centric sort of guy."

"Yeah, well…" Mogits hesitated, "they'll pay a bit extra—even if it's just in beer and bread—for me doing that. Maybe even sing about me in some story. Right, Goonthur?"

"Sure, mage," the barbarian clapped the smaller man on the shoulder, causing both the wizard and thief to stumble. "How'd you get back? Luna said you were dead."

"Reports of my death were greatly exaggerated. Not that certain parties didn't give it their best shot to make that happen." Mogits smiled at the priestess.

"You're not going to tell…" Luna trailed off, torn between anger and something else. Clenching her fist, she shifted her feet and looked away from the three men.

"It's simple…" Mogits looked at Goonthur and Manx, "Luna had to go because I had to run the magical thingamabob. The big, bad, box boy was rising from the flaming ashes of the tower, and I had to defend her as she ran away."

"I didn't run away!" Luna's voice rose to a shout.

"She's right, my apologies, I misspoke." Mogits gave a little bow of his head to the priestess. "She flew away, under my power and because of my sacrifice."

The woman glowered at the mage, but Manx's coughing cut the tension.

"I need to lie down," the thief said, "but I have to warn you, something's coming. Something big, and it's very, very dangerous."

"I know, kid," Mogits patted Manx's hand, walking forward, "but it's not coming here, and it's not coming tonight. So, let's go get some rest, and make plans to get back to the inn where we can claim our rewards…here and there."

"Yes!" Goonthur raised his voice to a triumphant shout, one hand patting the preening dragon on his shoulder. "We came, we saw, we stabbed many things. Now, it is time for wine, women, and song."

"Speaking of rewards…" Mogits looked at Luna, "thanks for bringing my bag of stuff with you to keep safe. I'll be taking that back once we're inside."

11. Epilogue

The rain beat down on the four travelers trudging up the muddy, rutted road. A steaming pile of horse manure in the gutter melted in the night storm as they approached The Traveller's Inn.

The weathered sign—an oval that was narrower at the sides, cut into a stylized shape that spoke of taverns, pubs, and inns for a long time past—creaked on three metal links, swinging in the constant breeze of the waning storm.

Goonthur's boots clumped on the warped boards of the porch. Moving further in, he looked over his shoulder and pulled off his cloak to shake it out. Water droplets flew in all directions, earning him a glare from Luna as she mounted the two steps.

Mogits slid around the woman, moving further down the porch where he could have more room to take off his outer wear. He hunched under the weight of his burden, the pack full of books. He'd had to share some things he'd acquired—assuring everyone he'd planned to do that all along.

Dropping his bag to a rocking chair, the thin man arched backwards, his fists planted firmly in the small of his back. Wincing, he groaned. A series of snapping pops came from behind him, and he sighed in relief.

"Where's Moist?" Goonthur asked.

"It's Manx," came a sigh from behind the barbarian.

The big man jumped, spinning in the air, and came down with a hand on the pommel of the sword at his waist.

"Don't do that!" Goonthur followed the admonishment with a few choice swear words.

"Stop calling me an adjective, and I'll stop appearing directly behind you where it would be so easy to find tender organs without you ever seeing the blade coming towards you." Manx smiled at the warrior.

"He's just so damned innocent!" Luna said, reaching for the handle of the door. "I mean, he's oily and sneaky, but that face has cheeks meant to be pinched. At least, it does when he smiles."

"Hey lady," Manx held up a finger, "remember the no touching rule?"

"You let that filthy, lying, conniving wizard touch you." Luna shot a dark look at Mogits.

"Yeah," the mage agreed, "but only after dark when the lights are out."

The thief snickered, and the priestess sighed.

Pushing the release on the door, Luna swung it open.

Looking around the warrior woman, Mogits noted the interior of the establishment looked slightly different from their last visit a few days ago. Was it the color of the sawdust? A new mirror behind the bar? Or did the stairs always turn at the corner of the ceiling? He couldn't put his finger on what it was, but something was definitely not kosher in Dodge.

A hush fell over the room, every head turning to look at the door, and the tinkle of the bell overhead cut through that lack of noise.

Luna stepped inside, pulling off her cloak and shaking it over the sawdust strewn floor, and reached to put it on a hook. Manx pushed past her, shoving the cloak out of his way.

"Why is it always like this?" the thief muttered. "She always blocks the door. Have some consideration for others. I mean, we've been walking in the rain for hours, and we all want to get inside and get dry."

"Because she likes the attention," the mage said loudly as he slid in on the other side of the warrior priestess, "likes people to look at her and check out her…"

Mogits fell quiet, chuckling to himself as Luna stared him down.

The three entered, each hanging their cloaks in various places, leaving Goonthur standing in the doorway. Blueberry ventured a look from behind the big man's calf, a look that spoke of an apprehensive child reluctant to return home.

The big man draped his cloak over his arm and gazed around the common room. He had a wistful smile on his face and looked relieved. Shifting the sword from his waist to his back, the barbarian then leaned down and unlaced his chaps. He only wore them in wet weather to stop chaffing. He also had a fur set for colder weather.

Mogits watched the warrior, the rain spattering and splashing in the puddles behind his bulked-out body. Goonthur looked contemplative, and…content. That was odd, at least for the barbarian.

Draping the chaps across the top of the wet cloak, the man entered The Traveller's Inn. He didn't shout, didn't bellow for service, or demand anything. He simply trailed after Luna and Manx as they meandered through the tables to one that was available.

It was the one in front of the fireplace, and Mogits saw Goonthur smile—just a little bit—but he saw it.

Luna fell into a chair at the head of the table, her back to the fireplace. Manx slid into the one to her left, his eyes shifting around the room. Goonthur settled into the one across from the thief, reaching to the center of the table to distribute the flatware and cloth napkins.

Mogits flipped a chair backwards, dropping onto it and

crossing his arms along the back, and setting his chin on his wrist.

A woman came over and Luna ordered for the group. Wine, mead, and ale, in addition to lamb, rye bread, veined cheese, and a vegetable stew would arrive shortly.

The mage looked around the inn, taking in the locals. At second glance, none of the people here looked all that local.

A gnome sat on a bar stool, glaring at the barbarian. No, not Goonthur, but Blueberry, who was curled up in the crook of the warrior's neck, nuzzling against him as the big man idly stroked her wing.

An ogre stood behind the gnome—no, not a full bred ogre, it had some other blood in it, it wasn't large enough for a full breed—patting the tiny man's back sympathetically.

A man in a swashbuckler's blouse lounged in a corner booth, one leg on the table in front of him, staring directly at the mage. He idly cleaned his fingernails with a stiletto, and a bushy-haired, rotund halfling stood on the bench beside him, animatedly gesturing as he told some tale.

Demon half-breed? Mogits thought, which was followed by a surprised realization. *How did I know he has demon blood in him?*

The glass-domed automaton that had been there before tended the bar. The thick golem with the broom leaned towards Cogsley, the whisper about the floors loud enough to be heard across the room.

Other patrons—like the crotchety man sitting beside the woman with the metal arm at the bar—stood out, but also blended in. The wizard wondered why he hadn't noticed their oddities on his previous visit.

The place had changed, and Mogits picked it out now that he could study the room. It was hard to focus on though, like the features kept slipping away from his awareness. Four other doors were on the exterior walls, as well.

"That's what's different!" Mogits gasped, almost to himself.

"What is?" Manx asked.

"Doors," the mage said without thinking, then clamped his lips tight.

"Yeah," Manx sighed, "I noticed two in the corners. You see them also?"

"Only one in the corner, but one on each of the main walls.

Mogits studied the kid. The street thief wasn't really a kid, far from it. If he would only shave off the sad wisps of a beard—maybe leave the moustache, but shape it with wax—and wash and cut his hair, he'd look like a man rather than a sulky youth. But the kid's eyes were sharp, and now slightly more haunted than they'd been when they'd left the establishment.

A cloth sack shinked onto the center of the table, the sound of moving coins pulling Mogits's attention from Manx to the reward dropped by Jack. All four of them jerked in surprise as the man appeared beside the table, Luna cutting off in mid-sentence as she explained the tenets of respect to Goonthur.

"Here's the designated payoff for your adventure," Jack said, smiling, "and I see no one needs limbs grown back or revived from a dead—or undead—state. That's great, you folks did okay!"

There was a chorus and thanks from the table, and Jack stepped to one side as the serving woman arrived with the food.

The group made appreciative noises at the trays, plates, pitchers, and trenchers set on the table. The woman departed and Jack centered himself again.

"Will you be staying long?" Jack asked.

"I need to be getting on in the morning," Luna said, pouring mead into her goblet, "but I'll need a room for the night."

Jack nodded and looked at the barbarian.

"I need to get back to my people," Goonthur smiled, "I think it would do me good."

"I'm sticking around," Manx said, not looking up as he ladled stew into his bowl. "This place looks interesting. Especially those new doors."

Jack raised his eyebrows, a smile teasing the sides of his mouth.

"I might hang out for a while too," Mogits said, "just to see what pops up."

"Something always does." Jack gave a small shrug. "Whether we want it to or not, it's never dull at the Traveller's Inn."

The Traveller's Inn

Travis I. Sivart

ABOUT THE AUTHOR

Travis I. Sivart writes Fantasy, Steampunk, Cyberpulp, Social DIY, and more. You can find him live streaming the writing and editing of his latest project from his home in Central Virginia, surrounded by too many cats.

You can find Travis on Amazon, Barnes and Noble, Books-A-Million, and other literary retailers.

Travis I. Sivart

Travis I. Sivart

Milton Keynes UK
Ingram Content Group UK Ltd.
UKHW010635040324
438885UK00001B/48

9 781954 214828